Revenge

Then to Slocum's shock, the woman brandished the .30-caliber and took off in a wild run toward the downed Comanches. Slocum rose and began to run after her. "Stop. They may be alive."

She never hesitated. She leaped and ran full out until she reached one. She aimed the pistol and struck him in the chest with the bullet.

"Stop. Stop," Slocum said. He caught her arm. She shook her head vehemently and then tore loose from his one-handed grip. Once free, she ran like a deer to another Comanche and shot him twice in the face.

Slocum caught her again. Still holding the rifle in his right hand, he smothered her to his chest. "Wait. Wait. You don't have to do this."

With amazing strength she managed to push her way free again and ran to stand over the third one. She emptied the .30-caliber into his chest. Screaming like an eagle, he died. Her arm hung limp, the smoking gun down at her side.

JAKE LOGAN

SLOCUM
AND THE WOMAN
SOLD TO THE COMANCHE

J

JOVE BOOKS, NEW YORK

THE BERKLEY PUBLISHING GROUP
Published by the Penguin Group
Penguin Group (USA) Inc.
375 Hudson Street, New York, New York 10014, USA
Penguin Group (Canada), 90 Eglinton Avenue East, Suite 700, Toronto, Ontario M4P 2Y3, Canada
(a division of Pearson Penguin Canada Inc.)
Penguin Books Ltd., 80 Strand, London WC2R 0RL, England
Penguin Group Ireland, 25 St. Stephen's Green, Dublin 2, Ireland (a division of Penguin Books Ltd.)
Penguin Group (Australia), 250 Camberwell Road, Camberwell, Victoria 3124, Australia
(a division of Pearson Australia Group Pty. Ltd.)
Penguin Books India Pvt. Ltd., 11 Community Centre, Panchsheel Park, New Delhi—110 017, India
Penguin Group (NZ), 67 Apollo Drive, Rosedale, North Shore 0632, New Zealand
(a division of Pearson New Zealand Ltd.)
Penguin Books (South Africa) (Pty.) Ltd., 24 Sturdee Avenue, Rosebank, Johannesburg 2196,
South Africa

Penguin Books Ltd., Registered Offices: 80 Strand, London WC2R 0RL, England

This is a work of fiction. Names, characters, places, and incidents either are the product of the author's imagination or are used fictitiously, and any resemblance to actual persons, living or dead, business establishments, events, or locales is entirely coincidental.

SLOCUM AND THE WOMAN SOLD TO THE COMANCHE

A Jove Book / published by arrangement with the author

PRINTING HISTORY
Jove edition / March 2010

Copyright © 2010 by Penguin Group (USA) Inc.
Cover illustration by Sergio Giovine.

ISBN: 978-0-515-14764-3

JOVE®
Jove Books are published by The Berkley Publishing Group,
a division of Penguin Group (USA) Inc.
375 Hudson Street, New York, New York 10014.
JOVE® is a registered trademark of Penguin Group (USA) Inc.
The "J" design is a trademark of Penguin Group (USA) Inc.

PRINTED IN THE UNITED STATES OF AMERICA

10 9 8 7 6 5 4 3 2 1

1

The one-eyed whiskey trader clumsily palmed a card while dealing the new hand. Seated cross-legged facing him in the lacy shade of a stunted mesquite, Slocum didn't miss his sloppy move.

"I don't know how the hell you're going to play six cards in a five-card game, but you better toss them all in and deal this hand over again. This time, be damn sure you don't try that trick again. You ain't playing poker with a drunk Indian, Kelso."

"Huh?" Kelso blinked his good eye at Slocum. The unshaven trader looked haggard to start with. His threadbare suit coat was covered in dust; his stovepipe hat had been smashed and had a bent top. He looked like a man who'd been riding drag on a cattle herd for weeks.

"You having trouble hearing me?" Slocum asked.

Kelso forced a grin. "Hell, no."

"What's her name?" Slocum indicated the woman in the buckskin dress, her hands and feet tied, lying on the filthy Navajo blanket with her eyes closed. Probably to shut out the fact of being Kelso's prisoner, which Slocum could imagine was, for her, like being in some kinda hell.

"Gawdamned if I know. She's white."

"How in the hell did you get her?"

"Whiskey. How else do I get things? Up on Prairie Dog Creek. I swapped with a couple young bucks—two barrels of whiskey for her."

"How long did they have her?"

"Who knows?"

"What's she worth?"

"Five hundred if I can find her family. I've got to get my expenses back."

"Get real. That damn rotgut you sell ain't worth a dime over twenty bucks a barrel."

When the cards were reshuffled, Kelso gave Slocum a grin with his tobacco-stained teeth, then began to deal again. "I've got her and they've got the damn lightning."

"What would you take for her?"

"Right here and the horse I been carrying her on?"

"Yes."

"Two-fifty and not a dime less."

"A whorehouse wouldn't pay that for her. You have no idea if she even has a relative left alive."

"What would *you* pay for her?"

"A hundred bucks. You personally can't stay around settlements for very long—anywhere. The damned army has your number. It would take a month or more, if you did locate her family, for them to get out here. By then, the army'd have your ass in irons and on your way to federal prison if they didn't shoot you."

Slocum looked at his new hand. Full house. Three kings and two tens. "I'll bet you a hundred bucks on this hand and you can use her for your collateral."

Kelso blinked at him. "Sumbitch, you must have a good hand."

"You playing or folding?"

Kelso studied his cards and nodded. "You got a deal, but she's my wager, no matter how high you want to go."

Slocum agreed with a nod.

Discarding two cards, Kelso drew two more and then grinned. "Wanta raise it?"

"Sure, another hundred."

"I've got it right over there." He tossed his head at her, and held up his cards like they were an ace-high royal flush. "What'cha got?"

"Full house, kings and tens." Slocum spread his hand out on the dirty blanket.

Kelso threw down his hand. "You suckered me into that bet—"

"You're over four foot tall and past twenty-one. Mrs. Whoever is mine." Slocum began to gather up his money and put it in his vest pocket.

"I had three eights and drew two deuces. What'cha going to do with her?" The silly grin on Kelso's face told Slocum what he was thinking about.

"She belongs to someone. I'm going to try to return her to them."

Kelso nodded woodenly. "Well, you screw her for me."

"I guess I'll be traveling on. Where's her horse?"

"That sorry bay."

Slocum rose and looked over the sparse Llano Estacado. The bay horse was a hundred feet or so away. Slocum rose, brushed off his butt, and reset his .44 and holster on his waist. Then he went over, bent down, cut the ropes around the woman's ankles, and then the ones around her wrists.

"Get up, gal. We're leaving."

She blinked blue eyes up at him in disbelief. Her face was caked with dirt. He wondered where he'd find enough water to give her a bath. She needed one badly. He hauled her up to her feet. She stood there numbly.

"Go catch that horse," he said.

Half staggering, she set out through the creosote brush, and he tightened up the cinch on his big roan gelding. She was the first woman he'd rescued in his life who didn't have something to say to him.

"She ever talk to you?" he asked Kelso, who was sulking, seated on the ground.

"No, but she damn sure tried to run away."

"She never said a word?" Slocum couldn't believe the man.

"No and I kinda liked that. I've had a few squaws in my time. They bitched all the damn time about something being wrong."

She'd caught the horse and was leading him back. Slocum climbed on the roan and went to help her. With his reata for a lead on the pony's neck, he bent down and made a stirrup out of both of his hands. She put her moccasin foot in it, and he loaded her on the bay. Still no expression on her face. He took the lead and went back to get his packhorse, a big Roman-nosed dun.

Ready to go, he went over to the whiskey trader. "I'll be seeing you, Kelso."

"Yeah. Next time you can rob me again, you sorry bastard."

"Just think, now you can go back to trading whiskey again." He turned to look back at the dull-eyed woman, who was holding a hunk of mane to stay on the mustang bareback. "We're leaving."

No reaction. So he left. He knew about a *cienaga* off to the southwest where water bubbled up in cattails, or tules as the Spanish called them. There were some pools of water there deep enough to give them both a bath, and he sure needed one as bad as she did.

A good bathing might bring her back to her senses. No telling. If she didn't talk, that would make it hard for him to ever find her people. But he'd try. She deserved that.

If she could talk, he imagined that she would have some bizarre stories about those bucks using her body for a prick cushion. Captives' stories were never nice, and obviously this woman had been subjected to plenty of abuse. Maybe her mind had simply retreated to escape the memories of their brutality—lots of women had reacted the same way.

It was near sundown when they reached the oasis. It wasn't paradise, but there were water holes in about forty acres of seeps, small pools, and a few gnarled cottonwoods, along with plenty of birds. The three horses, his roan, her bay, and the sorrel packhorse, filled up on water while he unloaded them one at a time.

She stood to the side and looked detached from everything. He didn't worry about her, and soon had his saddle and gear on the ground. In his saddlebags, he located a bar of soap along with two flour-sack towels, then moved over to her.

"You want a bath?"

No answer.

"Well, sister, we're going to take one." He set down his items and began to undo the ties on her leather skirt. She didn't stop him, and in minutes she was standing bare-assed in the long rays of sundown and he was lifting the buckskin blouse off over her head. Her pear-shaped breasts looked as dust-caked as the rest of her. She might have been younger than he'd thought before he undressed her. He'd thought she might be thirty, but he dropped his estimate five to seven years at the sight of her naked body.

As he shed his own clothing, her unresponsiveness bothered him—was she in shock, or had she lost her mind due to all the abuses she'd been through? He indicated the water, but she didn't move. So he swept her up in his arms, carried her over to the pool, and slid into the pool with a great splash.

She screamed and tried to climb over him. Her blue eyes were wide-open in fear as he forced her down in the water. "You won't drown. I won't let you. It is just water. There is nothing in here can hurt you."

With her squirming body held tight against him with his left arm, he pushed the hair back from her face so he could see her. "Take it easy. We're going to have a bath. And get all this west Texas dirt off of us."

He could still feel her shaking, and saw the jerky inhales of air she took. Using both his hands on her upper arms, he held her up in front of his face. "You will be safe. Safe. Do you savvy safe?"

No response.

"You screamed, damn it, so you can talk. Who are you, woman?"

She didn't even bat an eye.

He touched her chest with his index finger, and then pointed at her feet under the water to indicate she should stay there. She hugged her fine breasts, and he figured she understood that much. He scrambled up the bank and hurried over for his soap and towels. When he looked back, she was standing like a statue. At least she must have understood what he wanted.

Back in the pool, he began to scrub her skin with the soap. First her back, and when he finished, he put his hand on her head and forced her to kneel so he could rinse it. Then her arms and breasts—they were firm, and he felt some excitement while soaping them down. Then he rinsed away the soap by dunking her down again. He raised one of her legs and soaped it, then the other one. They were shapely legs, and the part of her body that had been under the skirt soon was snowy white like the rest of her body. With a a handful of suds, he worked her pubic area, and she widened her stance for him to go farther back. At last satisfied her crotch was clean, he made her squat down and he rinsed it with the same care he'd used to rinse the rest of her.

Then, he had her bend back and dip her head in the water. He went to work lathering her scalp, feeling the tangles and the rancid bear grease dissolving as he worked her hair with her chin deep in the pool. At last, the shoulder-length light brown hair was hanging wet and limp and, like the rest of her, was clean. To finish her off, he used a corner of a towel and gently washed her dust-caked face until her head and neck were clean.

She looked amazingly handsome. As she stood there without showing one shred of emotion, he wondered who she belonged to. Where had they kidnapped her from? He lathered his own body until he was snowy white with suds. When he finished, he dove underwater and came up with the remains of the soap dripping away. Crossing the pool and smiling at her, he held out his hand to help her up to the bank.

Instead, she threw her arms around him and hugged him. Then her hand caught his half-stiff dick and she tried to stick it inside her. He swept her up and carried her dripping out of the water to his bedroll. It was already untied, and he kicked it out like a carpet and carefully laid her down on top.

"I like women to say yes before I do this, but in your case I am excusing you." He took her face between his hands, bent over her, and kissed her softly. Then she pulled him down on top of her and spread her legs for him to come in between them.

On his knees, he eased the head of his fast-emerging erection in her gates, and she raised her knees higher for his entry. He moved slowly, for their fresh-washed skin was not slick yet with her juices. But it soon would be.

She was no stranger to sex, and he found himself enjoying her body. Even the look in her half-open eyes reflected the pleasure their coupling gave her. Her mouth soon opened she and showed her white teeth. She breathed deeper and deeper with grunting sounds coming from deep inside her throat as she strained to extract more from him. Inside her twat, she began to contract in spasms, and the urgency of their quest grew even more desperate. Finally, the tinkling in his balls began to signal the end was coming. When he strained hard into her, she clutched him, and they both climaxed in an explosion that drew all their strength away from them. Afterward, they collapsed in a heap, holding each other tight while he kissed her.

For a long while, they lay on the bedroll in each other's arms, enjoying their intimate moments as the western sky darkened. For a woman who'd been ravaged by horny bucks, she knew what she liked about having sex. The stiffness he'd felt earlier in her shoulders and back had relaxed, until her body resembled a slithering serpent that he could hug and squeeze as they enjoyed each other like newlyweds on the first night.

If only she could talk to him. Then, as he eased back inside her exchanging a knowing look with her, he realized he didn't care if she could talk or not. She was as tight and fine as any woman he knew. So he closed his eyes and pushed himself deep inside her. Damn, she felt good.

2

Job Toby sat his stout horse on the brink of the bluff and looked over the roundup operation in the open country beneath him. The Hendley brothers were taking a thousand head of his three-year-old steers to Kansas. Luther Hendley was overseeing his vaqueros, and the dust rose high in the sky as the cattle were sorted. This herd would soon be on the road, and his money problems would be over when they reached the railroad pens at Abilene, Kansas, in late summer. After the trail drive costs and sales expenses, he should realize as much as sixty thousand dollars—a sum he needed to settle some of his outstanding loans with the bank in Mason. They understood his strategy, and were willing to wait until then for their overdue loan to be paid off.

What he needed was the Texas courts to say that his wife, Juliana, taken by the damn Comanche over a year ago, was legally dead. Then he'd be free to marry Beth Ann Woolsey and silence her bitching about them living in sin. His plan to eliminate Juliana obviously had worked. He'd paid two tough Mexican pistoleros to kidnap her and then let her fall into the hands of the Comanche. Much better plan than murdering her and having the body to dispose of and lots of questions being asked.

First, if she had escaped the pistoleros, she would have had no proof he'd hired them. Second, not many women kidnapped by the Comanche ever came back alive because of the shame involved—usually they were pregnant or with a half-red kid in tow. No, by this time she was sprouting spring flowers out in that hell, and her late father's holdings, the entire 345 brand and ranch, would be his own at last. No way that bitch could have existed for long living on the Llano Estacado.

The cattle roundup looked well handled—they didn't need him. He rode off down through the hardwoods and cedar and crossed Live Oak Creek. Back in the cedars was a jacal, some chickens, and two hipshot burros. He dismounted with a cling of his spurs and searched around for sight of the woman—she was nowhere in view.

She must have heard his horse coming. He bent over and unbuckled his batwing chaps—taking his time. At last, he hung them over his saddle horn and strode to the house.

"Señor Toby—you—you surprised me," she said, moping her face on a cotton-sack towel in the doorway.

He stopped a few paces from her and looked at the short woman in her early twenties. "Take off your clothes."

"But—but—"

He waved her inside and looked disgusted. What was wrong with this bitch?

"What if my husband finds out?" Her fingers fumbled with the strings on her faded skirt's waist.

"So what? He needs the work on my ranch."

"But he would beat me if he learned I was fucking you."

"Take off your gawdamn clothes." He hung his hat on a wall peg and then frowned at her as he removed his vest and put it up.

"You don't have to shout at me." She sounded offended, but stepped out of the skirt to expose her short brown legs.

"Then do as I say."

"What if someone would come by while we do it?"

"Who would come by? Quit making excuses and get undressed."

She pulled the blouse over her head and exposed her rock-hard breasts with the pointed dark nipples as she struggled out of it. He took his shirt off, exposing his black hairy chest, and untied the gun belt and retied it so he could hang it close by on the post of the ladder-back chair. Then he unbuttoned his pants and motioned for her to come over. When she meekly approached him, he reached out and grabbed her, forcing her to her knees before him. Then, stepping out of his pants, he raised his limp dick in her face.

"Bring him to life."

She quickly took it in her hot mouth and began to work it over. As she grew more involved with her work, he ran his fingers through her thick hair and pulled her closer to his belly. He liked when she swallowed the entire length and his dick was deep in her throat with her lips on his pubic region. She could do it. Leya was one of the best at this in the entire hill country. There were women who screwed better, but she was the best when it came to sucking on his dick.

Her tongue was on fire working his shaft, and he felt stirred enough to come. She backed away, coughing on the creamy load that ran from the corners of her mouth. He simply squeezed her nose with an evil grin and forced her to swallow it. Then he hauled her over to the bed and bent her over the side so her small butt was in the air. With her small hand, she guided his erection into her twat. His thrusts began to move hard against her ass as he enjoyed the tightness of her pussy while giving her hell.

When he tired of that position, he drew out and tossed her up on the bed. With her knees beside her ears, he began poking her harder and faster. Her breath raged in and out of her throat. She looked at him and fainted.

"Damn you, bitch. Passing out on me." He was on his knees over her limp body. With his hand, he took a swipe at the juices flowing out of her gates and lubricated her rectum, flipped her over, then scooted up and inserted his dick in her ass. Groggy, she recovered, moaning softly until she regained speed.

"Oh, yes, oh," she cried out.

In seconds, he came again and this time he collapsed on her. Dizzy and done in, they spent the next hour kissing and playing with each other, his finger exploring her until she became worked up again. Breathing hard and straining against him while rubbing her erect clit as well, she soon came again and then sprawled out half unconscious on the bed.

He laughed at her lying there dizzy-eyed with drool running out of her mouth and her pussy as well. A mink in heat wasn't any match for Leya. Then he tasted her tits and feasted on them until he had a new half erection and shoved it to her. This time, they went much slower, and she finally finished him off with her mouth—complaining her pussy walls were on fire from his rough dick.

Dressed, he swept her up naked in his arms, kissing her hard and long, really enjoying her mouth and dreading having to part from her. Before going on his way, he left her eight ten-centavo coins on the table.

He reached the ranch near sundown, and saw someone hatless tied to one of the posts reserved for prisoners. The stable boy in the white clothing of a peon raced out to take his horse.

"*Señor patrón*, Valdez is waiting for you in the house." The youth took the reins.

"Who's he?" Toby asked, indicating the prisoner.

"A horse thief they caught this morning."

"Ah, Señor Toby," the well-dressed Raul Valdez said, coming to the front door under the pillared porch. "You at last return to *el rancho*."

"Cattle sorting went all right today?" Toby stopped in the shade of the two-story house and paused to look over the open meadow country to the east.

"Fine. We road-brand them tomorrow."

"This horse thief—" Toby indicated the man tied to a post.

"He was riding a 345 mare headed east. The boys stopped him and he had nothing to say."

"Nothing?"

"He won't talk."

Then we have no choice. Garrote him and then hang his body from a tree in the morning on the eastern edge of the ranch on the road to Decore."

"It will be taken care of."

Toby shifted the gun on his hip and went inside the house.

"Oh, Job, darling, you are home at last." Beth Ann came running into the room wearing her new red silk dress. "I was so afraid you'd miss the evening meal that everyone worked so hard preparing for you."

He kissed her pursed lips, recalling Leya's willing loose mouth only an hour earlier. A wife was never supposed to be a whore, but women like his bride-to-be could take lessons from whores like Leya on what a man really liked. But Leya was not the heir to a large Texas hill country ranch like the one Beth Ann's parents owned. Some day that ranch, like the 345, would be his, too.

While Colonel Walter Woolsey didn't particularly like his only daughter installed in the house of a once-married man, his spoiled daughter had won out and had moved to the 345 to await the court's verdict and their eventual marriage. And with Woolsey, who was well established in Texas politics, as an ally in Austin, Toby hoped that would speed the court's decision that his wife Juliana was legally deceased.

"I'm glad I am here, my dear, as well," he said.

One of the kitchen girls delivered him a glass of Kentucky whiskey and then curtsied for him.

"Thank you, my dear," he said, taking a sip to clear the dust from his throat. The liquor slid down through it like a road scraper, and he uttered a soft "ha."

"Well, today, Carmela had a fine baby boy." Beth Ann looked around to be certain they were alone. "I fear that her husband is not the father of this child. This boy is no doubt half white."

"Oh, lighter versions show up from time to time among these people."

She looked at the tall vaulted ceiling for help as they

strode arm in arm through the house to the dining room. "No, this is not that vaquero's baby. Someone else slipped in there."

"Who are we to judge?"

"Right."

The baby had been conceived shortly after the Indians took poor Juliana, and Carmela had been sleeping with him in those sad days, or rather nights, to comfort him over the loss of his dear wife. Carmela wasn't a mink in bed, but she was exciting enough to entertain him. Young and virginal, she had been a fine adventure while his plans moved forward toward taking on a second wife with a large ranch in her future. Then, when Carmela became pregnant with his child, Valdez handled the arrangements of her marriage to Manuel Vasquez, a boy her own age whom she liked. Then Toby and Carmela spent one last hell-raising night before she moved over to live in the row of jacales provided for the help.

Actually, he had picked out Beth Ann months before at a fancy social event at Fredericksburg, where the Texas Frontier Society met and had a social dance afterward. The TFS was led by some of the older men who'd fought in the Texas revolution, men like Colonel Woolsey. They had planned to form and support some Ranger companies, but that had never panned out since there was little money right after the war for anything. Still, men like Woolsey lived on like kings. This would be the second summer of cattle delivery to Kansas over the McCoy Trail to Abilene, and the summer before, it had worked extremely well—saving, no doubt, many fortunes stretched rawhide-tight by the long war and the following depression that had settled on the land. With Yankees in charge at the capital, and black soldiers ordering white folks around with bayonets, Texas had not been a happy or hopeful place—but the coming of the cattle drive had changed things fast.

One summer's money alone had things hopping. Toby had not forgotten his first dance with the lovely Beth Ann that evening. He had visualized himself feasting on her snowy breasts and then pumping his dick in her untested box. Waking up the beast under her smooth skin and coffered hair until she screamed for more. As he danced around to the waltz, his dick had grown harder and harder until he'd worried his condition might be exposed.

She'd known about his condition, which she'd caused. Several times during the fiddle music she'd brushed her lower body against him.

"I do swear, Job Toby, that you are some kind of a man," she'd whispered at the end of the dance.

"Thank you, my dear. Perhaps we can dance again sometime."

"I'd love it. Love it. Oh, there is Piper Jordan, I promised him a dance. Excuse me and, oh, tell your darling wife I appreciate her sharing you with me."

Beth Ann Woolsey knew damn good and well that she'd aroused him. Like you did before you bred a stallion. Get him all aroused over some lesser mare in heat, and then when his erection is up, slip in the blooded one for him to breed. That evening, he almost screwed Juliana to death, thinking all the time he was sticking it to Beth Ann Woolsey.

That death writ was bound to come out shortly.

3

They awoke naked and entwined in each other's arms. Slocum's sore lips were glued on her mouth as he kissed her hard. He'd found he was addicted to this woman's body. Kissing, squeezing, and screwing her had gone on and on all night until his brain was swirling and he felt drunk. Then he happened to see his blue roan gelding in the first light looking off at something in the east.

What was that horse watching? He put a hand on her bare shoulder. "I'll be back."

He dug his field glasses out of his saddlebags and searched the eastern horizon. Standing stark naked with the soft early morning wind sweeping his bare skin, he saw for an instant a lopsided stovepipe hat, and then feathers on the head of the next rider. Four bucks were either trailing them or had stumbled onto them. Kelso was not the one wearing that hat—this one had no beard.

She stood beside him as if waiting for him to speak. The first lances of golden sunshine were on her pear-shaped breasts. Damn Comanche anyway. They were disturbing his Eden. He'd better get dressed and serious.

"Comanche are out there. Maybe three or four young

16

bucks." He held up his fingers. For the first time, he thought she'd nodded. But her eyes were still awfully blank.

"We better get our clothes on and packed. They may have to work up courage to charge us. We need to be the hell out of here by then."

After they dressed, she tracked along beside him, and on seeing him saddling the packhorse, she did the same to his roan. When the horses were ready at last, she bellied up on hers, ready to go with a string in the horse's mouth for a rein. Slocum pointed northwest. Their next water would be the Pecos River, and it was a day and a half away.

He took a wary look over his shoulder, and saw no sign of the bucks. But his gut told him they were out there, and would be until they had her back and he was dead, or until those braves were dead themselves. A matter of who survived. She did remarkably well guiding the bay horse, and all Slocum had to do was point and she led the way. Her silence continued to bother him.

She could scream. But maybe she'd at last acknowledged with a nod something he'd asked her to do. He wasn't sure as they pushed their ponies northward exactly what he'd said. But she had answered him with a nod. He looked into the glaring sun coming up over the horizon, and thought about their hours spent making love in his bedroll.

Most white women would have put on something when they joined him looking through the field glasses. But being naked never bothered her. A lot of women he knew would have even dressed in the bed with him after they finished having sex. Not her. She became drunk on the excitement, and even afterward she enjoyed his attention in a relaxed, leisurely fashion. If she'd ever had a man before her kidnapping, he must really miss her every night when he climbed into his empty bed.

At noon, he was taking an old buffalo track beside a dry wash and keeping an eye on the horizon to the east. By trotting their horses, they'd made good time, but he knew for certain that they were not outdistancing the young bucks. If they would only expose themselves, he'd figure out a way to stop them. You needed to see your enemies to get a bead on them.

Obviously, these bucks knew that, too, and were staying out of sight. Besides, three ponies were no problem to follow, especially in this dry land. Nothing he could do about that. All he wanted was a fair chance to beat them in combat. With even odds, he could whip four young untried braves. They'd make enough mistakes from a lack of experience, and their brief hesitation would give him the edge in a fight.

Twice, he saw some fluttering in the brush at a distance. It was them. Though he only saw a dull flash of sun on a gun barrel or the turn of a horse's rump. There was someone there. And the infrequent presence of anyone in this land made the possibility strong that it was his war party.

Later that afternoon, a storm bank began to build off in the northwest. Dark, towering, ominous-looking clouds rose taller with the warming temperature. A strong spring thunderstorm was in the offing, and they were headed into it. It might be the best haven available in this brushy land. He sent a message to the powers above to bring it on—if they would.

He wanted to tell her he was doing all he could to avoid braves. Not because he was afraid of them, but because he didn't want her to fall into their hands again if he failed to defend her well enough. No use talking. She didn't talk back. That still bothered him. He reined the roan up and listened. He could hear the storm rumbling like a growling stomach. A few small wrens flitted nearby. Should he leave the buffalo road?

Storms like the one gathering up could push giant walls of water down through the land. In minutes, a trickle could become a flood. Higher ground was on a ridge east or west of where they rode. If the braves were skirting him on the east, then a flood might separate them. But he'd only seen occasional signs they might be there.

It was mid-afternoon and he shared some more jerky with her. They stopped only long enough to empty their bladders beside their animals, and then moved on. His Spencer repeating rifle was loaded to the gate with a tube of .50-caliber rounds. He had more ammo for the rifle. In the waist holster, his .44 Navy Colt cap-and-ball was loaded with five shots, with none under the hammer. He also carried a loaded .30-caliber small Colt in his right boot. That revolver was larger than a derringer, but much more effective than one.

That gave him lots of firepower. He could smell the rain coming. There really wasn't a good place to be. Not enough cover or anyplace to den up. He better make a decision, good or bad.

"Ride that way," he shouted as thunder crashed overhead. They'd be west of this dry draw and maybe separated from the war party. Penny-size hail began to pelt them. He undid a slicker and the large piece of canvas he'd used for a shade. Riding in close, he told her to put on the slicker, then deciding they'd gone as far as they needed to go, he slipped off the roan and began hobbling the horses as quickly as he could. Then, using the tarp for cover, he looked for her.

She quickly crowded in close as the tempo of the hail increased, drumming on his felt hat and shoulders under the tarp. The roar and force of the storm grew stronger, and he crouched down with her to get out of the north wind. Rain followed in heavy sheets and cut out light and vision. It was dark as night and the precipitation increased until it was hard to even breathe. He hugged her under the canvas that they held down on top of them, and she nodded her approval.

His boots were soaked and his hat must have weighed a ton. Water ran everywhere. With this much rain, the dry washes would soon be raging muddy rivers. Lightning illuminated their small world in flashes. Then the thunder cracked like a giant whip on top of them and made the ground under their soles shake.

When at last the storm waned, a low gray sky remained overhead. The temperature began to drop. He unhobbled the horses and they rode on. If the temperature kept falling, it would be snowing before dark. A late spring norther was rolling in, and there wasn't enough fuel in this land to build a good-sized bonfire. Sure would be pure hell to escape the damn Indians and then freeze to death in a spring snowstorm.

He didn't miss the mark by much. Soon, large flakes began to fall. He motioned for her to go on. In a few hours, the sun squeezed out and he made a rough camp in over a foot of snow.

Simply in case, he left the horses saddled. He knew they had lots of hard riding still to get off this caprock and find water and fuel. Those worthless bucks trailing them around, trying to prove they were men, should have stayed home in their tepees. Then he'd still be back there making tender love, not freezing his ass off out in the middle of nowhere.

He had some grain for the horses that he put in nose bags for them. He and the woman ate dry cheese and crackers. The tough jerky had made his teeth sore from gnawing on it all day. This had turned into more of a fix than he had ever imagined. They covered up the panniers and saddle, then kicked the snow away to put the bedroll down They unrolled the ground cloth and then put the larger canvas over the top. Finally, he put the rifle under the cover with them.

"This will have to do," he said to her as darkness settled in for the night and the snow continued to fall. So they didn't freeze to death, she was curled up in a ball against him.

Then, as if she couldn't stand it any longer, she rolled over and undid his pants. He raised up to let her shove them off his hips. Then her fingers began to knead his manhood and she raised up to kiss him.

Hellfire, this sure beat sleeping out here by himself.

4

Toby rode into town the following morning. Stuffed in his vest pocket he had a list of sundries that Beth Ann wanted. Being "almost married" to a little rich girl was trying on a man who had no time for such shit as buying some yellow thread and three yards of blue lace. Still, when he thought about her daddy's rich holdings, with plenty of water on the river, he could stand a lot to get all that land. Besides, she was back at the house and he was out in the world. He could have anything he wanted, and took whatever he desired when he wanted it.

He chuckled to himself. What Beth Ann didn't know wouldn't hurt her.

Decore was a small village on the Hurst Creek with a gristmill, a couple of saloons, some stores, two cafes and a parlor house on a side street in a two-story home that had once belonged to Doc Farley's widow. The doc had previously built a large barn on the property, so the neighbors didn't complain about the new owners, because a black stable boy put all the horses up out of sight in the barn. As a result, people weren't able to pass by this notorious house and see a familiar horse tied outside, and then go all over town gossiping about some leading citizen who was dipping his wick in some scandalous hussy's firebox.

He stopped first at Sam Pitch's Mercantile and left them Beth Ann's order to fill. Margie Pitch, Sam's thirty-year-old spinster daughter, came rushing down the aisle after him with the list in hand. "Does she want one- or two-inch-wide blue lace? Did she say?"

He looked hard into her brown eyes. "Better give me some of both. Then I won't be wrong, will I?"

"I'll do that. The back door will be open at noon," she said in a soft whisper.

The expression on her face never changed. He nodded with a small wink of approval. "Yes. Get me some of both kinds. Thank you, Margie."

"You are most welcome, Mr. Toby."

He went from there to the mill, and ordered a half ton of corn chops for his horses and mules from Elbert Gross. Elbert was standing in the warm spring sun, holding onto his overall suspenders while Toby was fixing to ride off. "I guess you're selling cattle in Kansas with them Hendley brothers."

Ready to remount, Toby paused. "Yeah, they're trail-branding 'em today."

"Just want to let you know, I'll be needing my money this fall, too. Your bill's getting kinda heavy to carry."

Toby pointed a finger at the man. "You'll be the first one I pay, Elbert Gross."

Gross simply nodded his head. "So I will be. So I will be."

Mounted on his horse, Toby held down his temper as he reined around and left. Why, the son of a bitch should be glad to be getting his business. He'd pay him all right. Damn that yokel from Arkansas anyway. Toby rode out on the road toward Mason, then past the last house, he opened a Texas-wire gate and headed up through Sam Pitch's mesquite and live oak pasture. Not seeing anyone, he cut off the hill and rode up behind the half-stone barn. A dairy calf inside bawled for his mother, who was off grazing on the wild onions and garlic. Garlic-tasting milk and butter. What a disgusting thought.

He hitched his horse in the back, rounded the barn, and slipped across the open area, easing himself up the porch steps and inside the back door. Pitch's wife had died a few years before, Pitch and his unmarried daughter of thirty lived in the big white two-story house. Toby had been fooling around secretly with Margie for years. She wasn't slender-bodied like his bride-to-be, but she had plenty of assets. He'd been eighteen the first time and she'd been twenty-three. He'd been working for her father—all by himself he'd been restacking the hay in the loft so the haulers could put more up there.

Margie came around in the afternoon and appraised him.

"I suppose you think you're a man," she said, coming up toward the loft a few more steps.

"Yeah, I'm a man. You woman enough to take on a real one?" He'd heard she'd told Ron Bartlett that sex was only for animals, one night when Bartlett had had her all worked up out behind the schoolhouse at a country dance.

"Put down that fork and come over here," she said. It was an order. He did as she said. He stood a head taller than her. When he was toe-to-toe with her, she reached up and jerked off his left suspender and then his right one. Gravity did the rest.

He had no underwear, so his dick and balls were exposed.

When he started to reach for his pants, she stopped him. "I thought you were a man."

"I am."

"Then why are you worried about your pants?"

He shrugged, feeling caught.

She reached out, captured his swinging dong in her fist, and began to jack him off. His first response was to scream, but he stuck it out there for her to handle. Run his rod out and jack it off till he came. And he finally did that, too.

She smiled at him. "Had enough, or are you man enough to do it again?"

He swallowed hard. "Let's do it again."

"All right, Mr. Big Dick, here we go."

Ha, she'd called him Big Dick. Her palm and fingers were rough from working in the store and the ranch, not soft like other teenaged girls who'd tried to jack him off. In no time, she had him breathing hard and straining against her rhythm. Then he let fly again.

Their foreheads were pressed together by then. "You said you was woman enough to take it. Now you get that damn skirt up and take your share."

Her brown eyes widened in disbelief. "You're serious?"

So he ended up inside her and almost never came the third time. She told him later he was the hardest-dick sumbitch she'd ever done it with. He said the same about her hand.

Now, he stood in the kitchen. They had a real pitcher pump in the sink. He took a mug with a handle and pumped up a few shots of water to get it cool, then filled his glass. The water went down good. Not as good as whiskey, but it wasn't gyp water either.

"Who's in my kitchen?" she asked, coming from the living room.

"You're early," he said.

"Business is slow today. I am taking a very long lunch hour break."

"Upstairs in your bed?"

"Where else? We aren't doing it in the hay ever again. I itched for months after that time years ago." She stood on her toes and kissed him. "How is your future wife?"

"Let's not talk about her." He swept her up in a hug and kissed her hard. "Let's talk about you and me." With his right hand, he squeezed her full left breast.

"What do we talk about anyway? How big your cock is? How big I am?"

"Listen, what you and I got most folks would bust a gut to have."

"We got—" She took him by the hand. "We've got lots of fun ahead today with you bouncing my ass on that bed."

"Remember that day in the barn?" He clapped her on the butt as he charged up the stairs behind her.

"Do I ever. I couldn't believe you could do that the second time, let alone the third time inside me."

Sunlight flooded the room from the tall windows. She undressed, spilling her large orange-sized boobs out and shedding the skirt off her ample hips until she stood naked before him. He stepped over and reached under her crotch to finger her twat. She moved her feet apart and his finger slipped in the pie. Of all the women he'd ever known, she liked being fingered better than most. His wife-to-be said it made her nervous and hurt her. Not Margie.

Soon, her clit began to grow erect, and she had a large one that responded easily. Almost like a miniature dick. It was big enough that he could jack it off and send her through the roof.

"Get on me, you horny bastard," she whispered, and then laughed out loud as he scrambled to obey. She was one good screw. He lathered it up in her hole until, after his third effort, she threw her arms aside and shook her quaking tits at him.

"I have to work the rest of the afternoon." Looking bleary-eyed, she laughed. "Three times. That's enough for any woman."

He left her in the room getting dressed. On the way out, he washed up his privates at the kitchen sink, dried himself, and searched around the yard before heading for the barn and his horse behind it.

He wasn't ready for the sight of the man with a bandage on his head sitting the spotted mule and waiting for him.

"Kelso Jennings, what in the fuck are you doing here?"

The man, looking weary, shook his bandaged head. "I thought I better come tell you I saw your wife alive five days ago."

"How could you have? She's alive?" Oh, damn, this was tough news. How could she have survived?

"Damn right she's alive. A little fucked up in the head, but she's alive."

"How do you know it's her?" He held out his hand to stay the man. "We can't talk here. Let's ride."

Kelso looked at the back of the house. "How long you been pitching it to her? She's Sam's daughter, ain't she? The one works in the store. Got tits like big oranges."

"Where were you?" Toby made sure no one was coming up or down the road. Then he got his horse and they made for the gate. When they were both outside, he restretched the wire gate.

"What's happened to her?" Toby mounted his horse.

"A fella on the lam named Slocum took her away from me. He's a tough sumbitch. Then I mixed it up with a Comanche war party and they beat me up pretty bad. Then they took off to find him."

"So what do you need?"

"Six barrels of whiskey for my troubles. I know you've got plans that don't include your last wife, like marrying that rich Woolsey bitch."

"Which way did they ride off?" Toby asked. His plans were none of this stinking whiskey man's damn business. He might need to poke a rag down his throat permanently.

"North, and I don't know why. If it was me, I'd of sure beat my ass to get to Fort Concho and turn her in."

Toby frowned at him. What did he mean by that? "I'm glad you don't still have her. Did she know you?"

"I think so. She tried to run away a couple of times. I had to keep her tied up. I figured she thought I'd bring her back to the Comanche and she'd be killed."

Toby sucked on an eyetooth as they jogged for town. He tried to figure what he should do next. "You did right. How much money you need to buy that rotgut?"

"Two hundred dollars, which ain't much. That'll buy it."

"They steal your hat, too?"

"They about got it all, but for this old spotted mule, and he'll kick the fire out of any Injun. He hates 'em."

"How long had this Slocum been gone when they struck you?"

"Just a few hours."

"You draw me a map. I'll go find 'em."

"I'm warning you, this Slocum's a killer. Them Comanche was all boys. But you better cock your pistol and be ready for Slocum. He's a mean sumbitch."

"You hear any word about her, you let me know."

"Where're you going?" Kelso asked.

"Soon as I get packed, I'm going looking for him."

"Buy me the whiskey, I'll go along and show you where I last saw him."

"You want six kegs?" He was low on cash and ever since they'd left the Pitch Ranch, he'd been trying to figure where in the hell he'd get that much whiskey, even rotgut, on credit until his cattle were sold.

"Yeah, yeah, I've got to have six kegs."

"Don't worry. I'll get it tonight. You be ready to ride in the morning." Damn, ordinarily, he'd've had the money to buy it—this would be tough. Probably cost him a good brood mare or two

"My pack mules are out at Waverly," said Kelso. "Where should I meet you in the morning?"

"That schoolhouse up there, around sunup. I'm certain there ain't any school being held right now. Bring your mules. I'll have the whiskey."

"You taking any pistoleros along?"

"I ain't certain."

Kelso shrugged. "See you then."

They parted at the crossroads and Toby headed for Chester Knowles's place. Knowles was a crook, bootlegger, and cutthroat, but he could get the whiskey. It was dealing with the fat bastard that bothered him the most.

He found Knowles half drunk, lying on a mattress on his front porch. He raised up on his elbows and looked bleary-eyed as Toby rode up. "What the hell do you want?"

Toby dismounted and hitched his horse to the wheel of the wagon parked close to the front stoop. "You."

"What for?"

Knowles's wife, Linzey, came to the doorway with her dress unbuttoned down the front, exposing even her deep navel and the dark patch of pubic hair below the slight swell of her belly. "Well," she drawled. "If it ain't the big man."

Linzey was fifteen years younger than her old man. And Toby knew her before they married. Knowles's first wife died having a baby. Then he took up with this wild mink from Slatter Creek. By Toby's reckoning, every horny boy in that county knew all the freckles on that girl's butt.

"Hi, Linzey."

"Get your ass inside," Knowles said, waving her back in the house. "Only reason he's here is to talk business."

She made a come-hither smile at Toby. "He may have come to see me." She flashed a long, small breast at him and then turned on her bare heel. "You don't know everything, Knowles."

"Come sit on the porch," said Knowles to Toby. "We can talk here." He scratched his belly, threw a leg over the side of the mattress, and reached for a crock jug. He removed the corncob stopper and took a deep swallow before he handed it to Toby.

"Ain't good, but it ain't too bad," said Knowles. "What the hell do you need?"

"I need to do a little swapping. I need six barrels of rot-gut whiskey and I've got some good brood mares bred to that roan stallion of mine to swap."

"Six barrels. What the fuck you going to do with that much whiskey?"

"That's my business. And I need them in the morning. Really tonight." Toby took a jolt of the liquid lightning and handed it back.

"Damn, that don't give me much time." Knowles took another snort.

"It's worth three good brood mares to me."

"Shit-fire, I'd have to ride my ass off to find that much whiskey."

"I'm talking three prime mares."

Knowles nodded. "I know them mares. They're the best bloodline around, but gawdamnit, that's lots of liquor and on such short notice." He dropped his chin. "I'll get dressed and go see what I can do. May take me all day. What if all I can get is four barrels?"

"Six is the deal."

"What else do you want?"

"My deal is six or nothing before daybreak."

"Shit. Linzey, get me a shirt. I got to go find some booze for this gentleman." He glanced up at Toby. "Make yourself at home here. I'll find the damn whiskey for you and be back here in a few hours. I ain't never reneged on a deal in my life." He went to scratching at the whiskers on the side of his face. "I'll get 'em."

Still with her dress open down the front, Linzey brought him out a shirt. It looked ironed. He undid his pants and spilled his privates out. Then he tucked the tail in and rebuttoned his fly. "Fix the man some lunch." He turned to Toby. "Bet you ain't ate."

"I'll do it," she said, and walked right by him, letting him look at all of her that he could see as she passed. "Take me a few minutes."

"Don't go to no trouble," Toby said.

Knowles offered Toby another tug on the jug. Then he took a big one for himself. The jug was on a rope so he could carry it along with him. Then he went and rode out in a jog on a spotted mule with an army saddle.

"You want food?" she asked from the doorway

"Sure," Toby said, with his mind on Knowles and wondering if the man could find the whiskey he needed. He better—

She took him by the hand leading him inside. "Job Toby, you're either pussy-whipped or in a trance. Hell, I'm walking around here half naked and you ain't even noticed me."

"I've got things on my mind," he said absently as she pulled him inside the dark house. Knowles was gone from sight going up through the live oak and cedar.

"Sit down and eat that food I fixed," she ordered. When he was seated, she got on her knees beside him and began to rub her hand over the bulge in his pants.

"I knew you had one." She threw her head back and shook the loose hair out of her face. Then she went back to playing with him as he forked in her fried potatoes.

"My, my, you sure ain't your usual self today. Why, I seen the time you'd've already been using my ass full steam. Undo them pants. I want to see that rascal."

"It ain't you, Linzey. I just got some business I have to tend to right now. I get some time in a few days, I'll be back over here and bang your ass real hard."

"Geez, I could use it today real bad, but if you promise."

"I sure promise."

In ten minutes, Toby was on his horse headed for his own place and not wasting any time. When he arrived at the ranch, he told the stable boy he wanted a packhorse ready before dawn and to load his bedroll on him. In the kitchen, he told Maria he'd need enough food for ten days and some utensils, and he wanted it all in panniers and ready to load on the packhorse before dawn the next morning.

Then he stormed around inside the house looking for Beth Ann. Where was she? At last, she appeared on the staircase. "You're home so early."

"I have business to tend to tomorrow. I may be gone for a few days." He kissed her cheek.

"What kind of business?"

"Business, business, my dear. I won't trouble you with little things."

"You are a dear, Job. Perhaps we will hear from the state court. I'd hate for our firstborn to be here and us not married."

"Oh, are you in a family way?"

"Well—not really yet. But I could be. Maybe we should try more often," she said in a hushed voice.

"Whatever. I was concerned that it annoyed you."

She clung to his arm. "Foolish boy, I love you. If I ever gave you that thought, it was totally wrong."

"Good, we can go up to our bedroom and try to get you in that condition right now."

She threw up her hand to cover her mouth. "But all the household help would know what we were doing, Oh, my."

He leaned close to her ear. "They do it, too—sometimes."

Slapping his arm, she asked, "Did you have lunch?"

"Yes."

"Good." Then she looked around before she said, "They will take a siesta shortly."

"Wonderful." He leaned over and spoke in her ear. "You go upstairs. Get naked and I will be up there shortly."

"Good. I will be waiting," she whispered, close to blushing.

"Fine. Where's Valdez?"

"I haven't seen him since this morning."

Damn, where was the man when he needed him? This Slocum was out there with Juliana. Toby would have lots of problems if she showed up—alive especially. He stormed off to the kitchen and asked Maria, "Where is my foreman?"

The woman shrugged and turned to the kitchen help. "Anyone seen Valdez this morning?"

The girls around the room turned up their palms or shook their heads.

Son of a bitch! Where had he gone? Toby hurried out the back door, and found the stable boy Hidalgo busy currying his saddle horse.

"Where is Valdez?"

"I have not seen him since early this morning, Señor."

Damnation, he needed to make plans to find Juliana and this Slocum. Maybe take along a few trusted men. Men that would not talk if he had to cut her throat when they found her. His complicated plans to deliver her to the Indians and let the Comanche kill her had obviously not worked. He should have killed her himself and said the Comanche did it. Then she would be dead and he would not be so damn upset about being exposed.

He looked back at the house. The help was retiring for siesta. His wife-to-be was waiting for him upstairs. He was so damn upset about this, he might not be able to raise a hard-on. Poor girl was such a loser in bed. Nothing like he was used to with Margie or the others. Even the skinny Linzey would have put out more than he'd find waiting upstairs.

Better get it over with and go find Valdez. He needed things ready to go by sunup. And Kelso Jennings knew too damn much—he might not live to come back from this hunt. Anyone who was a threat to Toby needed to be silenced. He'd see.

In the dark bedroom with the drapes drawn, he put his hat on the rack. "You are in here, my lover?"

"Yes," came the small voice from the bed.

He sat on the chair and shed his boots and spurs. "I could not find Valdez."

Then he rose and removed his vest, shirt, and pants. In the shadows, he could see her in bed with the sheet pulled up to her chin. As he moved to join her, all he could think about was the voluptuous Margie, who was like a great horse, so wonderful to ride. Or any of his other scattered lovers. Carmela, ah, yes, the one who had his son. She was very smooth in bed, too.

He lifted the cover and looked at the slender form. She tried not to, but she blushed as he scooted in.

"What is wrong? I am your husband. You are supposed to be glad when I come to share my love with you."

She raised up and hugged him hard. "Oh, Job, I guess I am just afraid. Perhaps when we are married—I—I will feel more at ease."

He kissed her and kissed her hard, tweaking her pointed nipples, and then ran his hand over the smooth skin of her belly. She finally moved her knees apart and he began to finger her. Each time he probed her, she flinched.

He frowned at her. "It hurts you, no?"

"Yes."

He removed his hand. It was no use. Carefully, he climbed over her thin legs and eased himself in the saddle gently and slowly. She lay back cold as ice and seemed anxious for him to be through. Soon he was.

5

That morning, before dawn cracked the eastern horizon, Slocum rose from under the covers and tarp. He put on his slicker and boots. Then the gun belt on his waist. He picked up the Spencer, wondering if he should take it or not. He finally decided to leave her the .30-caliber pistol from his boot.

If the Comanche killed him, she would at least have some defense. He hoped she didn't shoot him with it. He put the small Colt beside her hand, then scooted outside and left her sleeping. The snow made the tarp heavier to get out from under. He found almost a foot on the ground when he emerged into the starlit night. The three horses were standing hipshot, sleeping.

Good, he still had them. He surveyed the pearl landscape. No obvious sign of other horses, which would have stuck out over the low brush and grass stems. And no draws or rocks to hide them behind, so he felt better as the bitter north wind brushed his face. For warmth, the damn rubber slicker was worthless, but it did cut the breeze some. Wrapped in a few blankets, they'd make it through this late cold spell, but not without shivering some. A fire would be nice, but any cow or buffalo chips they found under the snow for fuel would be damp enough not to burn. There would only be smoke.

He was anxious to find an outpost. A hot stove to roast his fingers at and a boiling-hot meal. He didn't want much, he realized, carrying the rifle in his arms and looking for any sign of the red devils in the snowy landscape. Satisfied as he could be about not seeing them, he turned and went back to saddle the horses and move out.

When the sun climbed over the eastern ridgeline and shot red-orange spears across the snowy crust of the earth, they were moving out. The back of his neck itched the whole morning as they crossed the fast-melting snow. Although the temperature wasn't rising very fast, it was warmer than freezing and the solar heat was reducing the white stuff.

He wished she could talk. Her obedience to his unspoken plans made him feel uncomfortable. Twisting in the saddle, he saw nothing, but that didn't mean the braves were gone. Comanche were masters of hiding and popping up when you least expected. Someone to talk to could be comforting, even someone as wild in the blankets.

Late afternoon, he jerked up from being half asleep. His horse had seen something, and he saw it, too. Four bucks armed with rifles, screaming like half-mad coyotes, were coming off the ridge to the right.

He spurred up beside her and dismounted, handing her the reins to his horse and packhorse lead. She quickly slipped off her horse and looked concerned.

"Don't worry." He levered a cartridge in the Spencer. He knelt down and, looking through the sight, held his fire until he knew his bullets would count. She tapped him on the shoulder and he looked around at her. In her hands, she held a half dozen tubes filled with cartridges for his gun that had come from the packhorse.

He nodded and went back to sighting in on the braves. A war-painted buck in the lead rode a piebald horse. That was the one that needed stopping. Using all the elevation he dared, he squeezed the trigger. The black powder smoke from the muzzle swept over his face, burning his eyes. But the black and white horse went nose-down, then end over end.

Levering in a new round, he noticed the excitement written on the woman's face as she squatted beside him. All he'd seen was the rider flying off into the snow. He never got up. That lowered the count to three. The braves pushed on, screaming loud enough to unnerve anyone in hearing. He tried to ignore their high-pitched screaming as they came on, riding low on their horses' backs, waving what looked like some single-shot trader rifles. With the second buck in his sights, he shot, and must have missed, because they all kept on coming. A new round in, a new shot. The rider, hard hit, threw his hands in the air, lost his gun, and fell off the rump of his spotted horse. The paint then shied into another rider and unseated him.

The last one on horseback veered to the right and, despite two shots from Slocum's Spencer sent after him, rode off unscathed in a snow-flinging race to the north.

Then, to Slocum's shock, the woman brandished the .30-caliber and took off in a wild run toward the downed bucks. He rose and began to run after her. "Stop, they may be alive."

She never hesitated. She leaped over some bushes and then ran full out until she reached the buck who'd been unseated. She aimed the pistol and struck him in the chest with the bullet.

"Stop, stop," he said. Slocum finally caught her. She shook her head vehemently and then tore loose from his one-handed grip. Once free, she ran like a deer to another buck, lying on the ground moaning, and shot him twice in the face.

Slocum caught her again. Still holding the rifle in his right hand, he smothered her to his chest. "Wait. Wait. You don't have to do this."

She looked out of her hooded eyes at him and with amazing strength, managed to push her way free again. She stumbled getting loose, but quickly recovered and ran to stand over the third one. She emptied the .30-caliber into his chest. Screaming like an eagle, he died. Her arm hung limp, the smoking gun down at her side.

He took the revolver from her and stuck it in his waistband. The barrel radiated heat against his lower belly.

"You know them?" he asked, holding her against his chest.

No answer.

But he knew. She'd been in severe bondage to them. Their captive, to be used as it suited them. Horny young men who intended to torture their enemy. To make her less than a human. Even dogs were treated better than women slaves, and Indians ate the dogs. Holding her as she sobbed freely on his vest, he looked off to the north for any sign of the fourth buck. He must be long gone.

The next day, he saw the flag waving on the distant flagpole. He soon learned it wasn't an army outpost, but a trading post run by a bearded older man named Ersham Woodberry. The flag represented the new nation of Cally, whatever that meant. It was civilization in a raw form and there was water, food, plus at least one heating stove. In the sharp wind, traces of the smoke from the rusty tin pipe carried the sharpness of mesquite burning.

At their arrival in front of the low-roofed main adobe building, Slocum dismounted, swept off his blanket cloak, and tied it on the saddle with rawhide lacing. That task completed, he went over, took the woman in his arms, and lifted her off the horse. Holding her tight, he kissed her cheek and whispered in her ear, "Have no fear. I'll protect you."

No reply.

Out of habit, he shifted the Colt on his hip. Then he led her by the arm to the doorway, which was covered with a buffalo hide. Raising the hide and pushing it aside, he sent her inside and followed, allowing the skin to flap back in place. He let his eyes adjust to the room's shadowy darkness illuminated by a few candles. The main feature was the stove, and he guided her toward the radiant warmth already reaching out to heat his face.

"Feels good, don't it?" a gravelly voice demanded. His grizzly face, thick beard, and piercing dark eyes carried an authority about them. "See you got better company this time." He motioned to the woman. "Lots better looking." Then Woodberry cackled.

Slocum nodded. "She sure is." He noted the three men in cowboy garb at the card table to the side, and several solemn-faced Indians under trade blankets seated back at the walls in the darker portion of the room.

The man shuffling cards under the high-crown hat asked, "What brings you and your lady to this godforsaken place?"

"A little shelter and rest before we push on."

"Hell, boys," the man said, beginning to deal. "She ain't no two-bit squaw. She's a white woman under that garb."

The freckle-faced younger one grinned and tipped his hat to her. "Howdy, ma'am. Geez-oh-Jesse, I ain't seen a woman that good-looking in years."

"Kid, you'd think a greased-up ewe would look good."

"Where's one at?" Freckles acted like he was ready to jump up and go after it.

Slocum ignored them and went to the bar.

"What'cha drinking?" Woodberry asked.

"We'd rather have some hot food."

"I got frijoles on the stove."

"We'll take two large bowls."

"Want some tortillas?"

"Fresh?" Slocum asked.

"Pretty fresh." Woodberry acted fascinated by the woman. "You like frijoles?" he asked her.

"She doesn't talk," Slocum said. "I'm sure she'd like anything but jerky. We've had a steady diet of it."

"She a deaf mute?"

"I don't think so. Simply don't talk. Dish up the frijoles."

"She been like that long?"

"Long as I've known her."

Woodberry went to fill the tin plates with his frijoles from an iron pot on the potbellied stove. He used a wooden spoon to mound them up, and handed one plate to him and the other to her.

Then he indicated a two-chair table near the stove. "I'll bring the tortillas and what to drink?"

"You have fresh coffee?"

"It was made a while ago."

"We'll try it."

"I ain't got any milk."

"Don't matter."

Soon, they ate in silence except for the three cardplayers, who made comments about how they hadn't been that close to a real white woman in a long time.

"What's the going price in Fort Worth for a woman like her, Earl?" Rudy, the third one, asked the dealer.

"Ten bucks I'd say, Rudy."

"That for all night?" Rudy held up his cards, obviously to see his hand better in the darkness back there.

"That's for fifteen minutes, brother. You going to bet?"

"Yeah, two cents."

"Make it a nickel," Earl said.

"You're expensive as some Fort Worth dove to play cards with."

The freckle-faced younger one turned to Slocum and the woman. "Mister, I never caught you all's name. I'm Freckles Cole. That's Earl Simpson and the old geezer is Rudy."

"Slocum's mine," he said, filling the tortilla with beans. "She don't have a name."

"No name?" Freckles looked astounded at the other two. "No name."

"No name."

"Holy cow, no name. Where did you get her?"

"From a whiskey trader in a card game."

"You boys listening to that?" Freckles asked them. They nodded with their cards on the table. "How did you get so lucky?"

"I drew a good hand. We were playing for a hundred bucks. I had the money, he had her for his part of the ante, and he lost."

Freckles narrowed his green eyes as if pained. "Damn, you bought her for a hundred bucks?"

Slocum nodded. "And she ain't for sale."

"That's a shame. What'cha going to do with her, like I don't know?" Freckles snickered.

"Return her to her people if she has any."

"But she ain't talking."

"Ain't said a word in four days." The frijoles weren't stale. The tortillas were a little dry, but she ate them like they were good. Hot coffee cut the scum out of his throat. At that point, he decided he might live, and shared a bright-eyed look with her. "That wasn't half bad, was it?"

No reply.

"If you wouldn't sell her, would you rent her at Fort Worth prices?" Rudy asked. "I'd gawdamn sure pay that much for some time in her bed."

"No."

"Double them prices?"

Slocum shook his head.

"I don't know why not. She don't talk. Who's she going to tell?" Earl asked, scoffing at him.

"She's my ward and I'm taking her home."

"But you said—"

"Woodberry, you got a jacal for rent?" Slocum asked the man behind the bar.

"Sure, fifty cents a day." The man grinned behind his beard.

"That's higher than the Palace Hotel."

"I got fancy jacales."

"Two nights. How much is the food?"

"Fifty cents."

Slocum walked over and put the money on the counter. "Which one?"

"The back one."

"I have three horses that need feed and water?"

"Another dollar. I'm letting you off light. They charge the hell out of me to bring hay to this place."

Slocum paid the man.

"Don't screw her any more than I would," Freckles said. The three sour faces went back to playing cards.

If she'd been any other woman and he'd said that, Slocum would've kicked the shit out of that boy. Instead, he shrugged Freckles's comment off as she pulled on his sleeve to get him to leave the place.

Outside, the sharp north wind reminded him that the last storm of winter was still on top of them. They led the horses to the last jacal, then unloaded and unsaddled them, taking all the supplies inside. Before he went to put the horses up, he dug out three matches and pointed at the fireplace with the split wood beside it.

She took the matches from him and turned toward it. He shrugged, satisfied that she understood, and went out in the twilight to put the three horses in the pen and be certain they got water and hay. At the pump, he worked the handle, filling the trough for the thirsty horses. He was so intent on the job, he never heard anyone slip up behind him and clobber him over the head.

The lights went out.

6

Valdez came in about twilight and reported to the house. He met Toby out in the hallway to talk in soft tones about a cattle deal.

"They have our man in jail below the border."

"Sanchez?"

Valdez nodded. "It will cost a hundred pesos to get him out. I am afraid, Señor, if we don't get him out, he may talk. Then we could all be in trouble."

"Texas has never enforced Mexican law for them."

"But now we have a carpetbagger government. They hate Texans. What better way to show their power than turn some Texas ranchers over to the Mexican government for rustling in Mexico."

"You know how short on money I am today. I traded that damn Knowles three good ranch brood mares for some whiskey to pay Kelso today." Toby lowered his voice. "Kelso says that my wife is alive and with some sumbitch named Slocum."

"Where are they?"

"He's going to show me where he was when this Slocum took her away from him. Kelso had got her off some Comanche bucks."

41

"Caramba!" Valdez slapped his forehead. "That is worse news."

"Think how we can raise the hundred dollars, and I want two tough men to ride with me. You go to Mexico and get our man out of jail. I'll finish this other deal once and for all."

"Take Polo and Guerra with you. They are the best pistoleros."

"Can you think of any way to raise the hundred dollars? Money is tighter than a bull ass in fly time in Texas."

"Gardner Phillips will loan it to you."

Toby gave a hard frown at his man. "At a hundred percent interest?"

Valdez turned up his palms at him.

"Ride over there tonight and get the money," said Toby. "I will write a note for you to give to Phillips. Tell Polo and Guerra they must ride to Knowles to get the whiskey and take an extra boy to bring those spare packhorses back. I'll be meeting them and Kelso at the Waverly Schoolhouse at dawn. He'll have mules to transfer it to."

His foreman began listing things he'd need. "You will need bedrolls, cooking gear, food—for how long?"

"Two weeks, I hope."

"You will need four packhorses for that stuff."

"We have them. I guess you're right, but I'd really wanted to travel lighter and told Maria so."

"But there is nothing out there."

Toby looked at the ceiling for help. "You're right. Nothing but her. Gawdamn her."

"Have you talked to Maria about all this?"

"Not that much."

"Then I will tell her about the supplies you'll need. I will send the men after the whiskey. And then ride to Phillips myself. What about Knowles and the mares?"

"He can come choose them anytime. Send him word when you get back. He can come over if I've not returned by then."

"I can handle that." Valdez laid a hand on Toby's shoulder. "You, *mi amigo*, must be very careful. You have a dangerous job ahead of you. Dealing with Kelso Jennings is one thing, but anyone that he fears is a tough hombre."

Toby would probably leave that whiskey trader for the buzzards to chew on when all this was over. Kelso knew too much—way too much to be walking around. If Toby's plan was that obvious, others knew about it, too. But proving it, as long as Juliana wasn't there to testify, would be impossible.

He sent word with the maid for Maria to wake him up at three o'clock, and then took his wife-to-be up to bed. When she climbed in bed, he wet his fingers with spit, lubricated his tool, raised up, moved between her bird legs, lifted her nightgown, and pushed it into her. When that job was over, he fell fast asleep.

His wake up call at three in the morning caused her to stir. But she never fully woke up.

"When will you be back?" she muttered.

"When I get through with my business. Go to sleep."

"I'll miss you, my darling."

Miss what? He'd not miss *her*. The other women in the world he'd slept with he would miss—yes. She was either the coldest or the dumbest woman that he'd ever had relations with in his life. One time he'd climbed in bed with a grandmother who was way over fifty years old, and she was much hotter in bed than Beth Ann ever was.

Dressed, he bent over and kissed her. "I will hurry back, but don't fret. It may require several days, or weeks even."

In the kitchen, he gobbled down the food Maria had ready for him to eat, and when finished, he struck out for the corrals. With his own best horse and four packhorses, he left in the cool air. It had lightly snowed a few days before, way too late for that time of year, but he wore a heavy wool coat just in case it happened again.

Kelso was waiting for him. Cloaked in a wool blanket, he was pacing back and forth. The mules were loaded and the boy was ready to ride for the 345 with the extra packhorses. Polo and Guerra were close-mouthed, and nodded when he rode over. The short young men were in their early twenties. Valdez said they would be good under gunfire. Toby hoped so. But no man walked the earth that he trusted more than his foreman. Valdez knew men and had never been wrong in his appraisal of employees.

Toby stepped down and spoke softly. "Either of you know a man named Slocum?"

They shook their heads.

"He's who we're going after. They say he is a very tough hombre, but there's three of us—we'll get him."

Both nodded as if to show that would not be a problem. He finished tightening his girth and slapped down the stirrup. Those damn braying mules would make him want to kill every one of them before this ordeal was over.

"Let's get the hell out of here," he said, and they rode away.

It took two days for them to reach the site of the ambush. The tracks were faint, diluted by the snowfall that had since disappeared. Polo found enough track to lead them north the next day. On the second day, they found buzzards feasting on three dead Comanche.

Polo, Guerra, Kelso, and Toby sat on their haunches in a half circle to discuss their discovery and make plans.

"Boys," Toby began, "them bucks were shot at close range. Maybe to finish them off. You recall that piebald lying over there, Kelso?" He looked over at the trader for his answer.

"Yeah, damn right. These were the ones I bought her off of. The leader rode that horse. But there was four of 'em back then."

"If there were four, who got away here?" Toby asked.

"I think the youngest. One Who Whistles. We may find his body on this road. Which way did he head out of here?"

"We think he rode north." Polo waved his hand in that direction.

"No telling," Kelso said, shaking his head as if stumped by their discovery. "He killed them all in a small area around here. I told you that bastard Slocum was mean."

Bullshit. Toby had a bullet for him, too. "You think they rode north after this?" he asked his two men, who seemed to know this tracking business.

"They went north," Guerra said.

Polo agreed.

"Let's ride. I like sleeping in my own bed. Sooner we get them, the sooner we can go home."

Both men vaulted on their horses. It was another day before they saw Woodberry's flag at the fort waving.

"What in hell's that?" Toby asked Kelso.

"Woodberry's national flag."

"What the hell does he call his nation?" Toby checked his horse.

"Cally. It was after some whore that he used to have."

"Maybe he knows where the hell Slocum went."

Kelso was slow answering. "He's a tough old fucker and he'll only tell you what he wants you to know. Watch him."

Toby nodded and booted his horse toward the fort. That old sumbitch wouldn't be so tough when Toby got through with him.

7

Slocum woke up soaking wet, and through his blurry vision could see, in the starlight, Woodberry standing over him holding a bucket.

"I thought they'd kilt ya."

Wiping his cold wet face and trying to see better, Slocum grimaced at the thoughts in his pounding head. *They'd gotten her*.

Using the trough for support, at last he managed to stand up. Shaking his head, still in shock over the attack and kidnapping, he shivered. Then he swept up his hat and followed the man.

"Come on inside," said Woodberry. "I got some real good whiskey. You need some. I didn't figure out what they were up to in time or I'd've tried to stop them. They split up and I thought two of them went to the outhouse. Turns out they conked you on the head and took her instead."

"Where they going?"

"New Mexico, I guess. They robbed some fella in Kansas. I guess he had a helluva lot of money on him, but they figured he'd hire Pinkerton to get on their asses. So they were trying to leave no tracks."

"Who was the fella they robbed?"

"Burleson? That sound right?" Woodberry pulled the buffalo hide aside for him to go inside the trading post.

"There's a Burnett Burleson. He's a big cattle dealer in San Antonio."

Woodberry went behind the bar and set up two glasses. Then, using his pocketknife, he cut the seal on the bottle and popped the cork. He sniffed it. "You smell it. This is damn good whiskey."

After sniffing, Slocum bent over and felt his boot top. At least they hadn't gotten his money. "You see my horses?"

"Yeah, they didn't steal them. Why?"

Slocum raised the glass and looked at the brown liquor, "'Cause I'm going after them and let the buzzards eat their worthless hides."

Then he downed the double shot. It cleared the Texas dust out of his throat and warmed his ears. He set the glass back on the bar, then used both hands on the rounded edge to brace himself. "I need to eat something, then I'll pack and ride."

"You better wait a few hours until your head clears. You get out there and pass out in the saddle, and the buzzards will eat you."

Slocum considered the man's words. "All right. I'll go try to sleep a few hours."

"There's a boy around here. He won't cost you much. He would tend to your horses, cook, and look out for you. He wouldn't be any extra baggage. But four eyes are better than two."

"What is he?"

"A breed. An outcast. But he's gritty and needs a chance."

Slocum looked at the dusty bottles in front of the imperfect mirror back of the bar. Maybe not such a bad idea. "Have him here at sunup. What's his name?"

"Carlos."

Shaking his head at Woodberry's offer to pour him more whiskey, he went outside, caught his horses, and put them in the pen. His still-wet shirt and vest about froze him in the sharp wind, and once in the jacal, he hung them up. Maybe they'd dry overnight. He soon found the bedroll blankets were really cold without her body heat next to him. He rolled over on his belly, and soon fell into a troubled sleep.

He had bad dreams about that freckle-faced outlaw torturing her for his own pleasure. He awoke in a cold sweat and blinked at the silhouette of a boy under a serape squatting—waiting.

"You Carlos?"

"Yes, sir."

"Well, we need a fire to cook something." He reared up and produced three matches. "Warm this place up."

"Yes, sir." The boy rose and went to the fireplace. In a matter of minutes, he had the fire going.

"How did you do that?" He sat on his bedroll pulling on his boots.

Carlos shrugged. "The fire was made, but no one lit it."

Slocum nodded, recalling telling her to start a fire. "She did that—before they kidnapped her."

"This is the pretty lady that was at the store last night?"

"She has no name. She can't talk. Between bad treatment by the damn Comanche and a whiskey trader, I think she lost part of her mind."

"How will you get her back?"

"You and me are going to track those bastards to the end of the earth. Until we find them. Then we're taking her back."

"How will I help you?"

"I'll find or buy you a gun and teach you how to use it."

The boy's brown eyes lit up. "Si, Señor, that would be *muy grande.*"

"All right. We've got that settled. Now what the hell're we going to cook?"

"I can cook. Let me look in your packs."

"Find us something. I'll go get the horses."

"They are outside. I already curried them down."

He looked hard at the boy. "You ever sleep?"

"Not since he told me you had work for me."

Slocum laughed. "I guess there aren't many jobs around here, are there?"

"No, sir."

"I'll start saddling. You start cooking." He slapped on his hat. "We'll make a good outfit, and them three worthless skunks will rue the day they took her."

"Yes, they will."

The boy cooked oatmeal with "bugs." It had plenty of raisins in it and brown sugar, and Slocum nodded in appreciation. There was enough for two bowls apiece, and he felt full and satisfied for the first time in weeks. "It was good. Now I don't have a saddle for that horse."

"I can ride bareback. It is much better than walking."

"Good. I aimed to find a saddle for her. I should have taken one of them Comanche saddles, but we never thought about that. Lots that I never thought about. Those three fellas acted tough enough, but I never figured they'd knock me over the head and take her. So much for my appraisal of men."

When the dishes were washed, they set out as the sun made golden spears over the horizon. The air was cold enough that their breath came out in clouds. Wrapped in blankets, they rode west on the tracks that Carlos said were the three men's prints. The day began to warm and the south wind grew stronger. They trotted their horses hard. Looked like those three men had four spare horses and were riding equally hard out ahead.

That evening they reached a jacal and pole pens under some cottonwoods that were showing small leaves. Obviously there was water there. When they reined up, a short Mexican woman came out in the bloody sunset light and looked at them hard. She spoke in Spanish.

"To water a horse is a quarter, feed is also a quarter."

Slocum nodded. "You have food for us?"

"It is also a quarter."

"Were three men and a woman through here today?"

"Yes."

"Did they mistreat her when they were here?"

"Yes."

"How?"

"Like they did me."

Slocum swung down. "They raped you?"

"And her, too."

He removed his hat. "I am sorry we came too late."

She shrugged. "They did not get a virgin. But if they ride by here again, I will kill some of them."

"They ain't riding anywhere if I catch them." He put his arm on her shoulder and hugged her. "Where is your man?"

"In old Mexico. He is off on some business, huh?"

"What is your name?"

"They call me Dominga."

"You have coffee or tea?"

"*Sí,* plenty for you, big man." She clung to his hand on her shoulder.

Slocum looked over at the boy, who was already busy unsaddling, and nodded his approval. The boy would be all right. Woodberry did Slocum a favor giving him Carlos.

Inside the jacal, she pulled his face down and kissed him. "I am not a *puta,* Señor."

"I know, and men like those bastards respect nothing."

"Nothing. It is one thing," she said, pouring hot water in a cup, then shaving tea off a bar in to the cup, "one thing to lie with a man when both are willing to make love. But when a man pulls my hair, slams me around, and then pokes his dick in me, I want to vomit on him."

"Who did that?"

She indicated he should sit on the Navajo rug.

"Was his name Earl?"

She nodded.

She used a wooden dowel to get honey out of a small tin bucket, and then swirled the tool in the tea so it clunked on the side of the cup. "Here. Now drink my special tea and we can talk of nicer things."

She sat on his lap with her small hand on his neck. He kissed her and then he sipped the tea. "Wonderful."

"Will that boy come in on us?"

"No."

"Then we can use a few minutes for ourselves. I need

someone gentle to hold me and act like I am more than some bitch in heat." She closed her long lashes and squeezed her eyes shut.

Soon, she stole his hand and shoved it under her blouse. He felt the small breast capped with a rock-hard tip, and massaged her nipples until she rose to kiss him harder. With her fingers, she undid the strings on the side of her skirt and shoved it down so his hand could slide between her legs. She widened her stance, and he soon probed his middle finger inside her.

Her tongue began to search his mouth, and her breathing became as heavy as his. He carried her to the pallet and quickly shed his clothes. Then he went under the covers to find her, for the room was cooling into the darkness. With care, he moved over her small body, and her legs opened wide so he could insert his erection. The sharp talons of her fingernails bit into his shoulders, and soon raked his back as he hunched it to her. They fell into a whirlpool of pleasure, and soon they came. Then, lying exhausted in each other's arms, they rested.

Later that evening, she cooked them a supper of goat, cheese, and spicy beans. Her food was as wonderful as the oatmeal, or better. The boy wiped his greasy lips on the back of his hand and grinned at Slocum. "Good food, huh?"

"Yes." Slocum agreed, but despite Dominga's good food and company, he was eaten up with his concern for the poor woman captive being dragged around and abused by the three men. She'd be lucky to have any mind left.

"Did they say where they were going?" he asked Dominga.

"They mentioned New Mexico."

He nodded. "That's a big place."

She agreed. "How will you find them?"

"My guide Carlos here can track a mouse over a rock," he said.

She smiled for his sake. "But they are ruthless men."

"So are we," he said with a firm nod. If he ever caught

up with them, he'd show them some of their own medicine. It was the catching up that was the hard part right now. The three had a good day's head start on him, and he felt certain they knew he was coming up their back trail.

"Dominga, we need to get up very early and catch them," he said.

"I will wake you before the chickens even stir."

"You are a fine hostess. Your food is the best and I can only apologize for those men."

She almost blushed and nodded. "I never expected anyone like you to be after them. All who stop here are outlaws and renegades who have no respect for anyone or anything."

Slocum slept with the woman on her pallet, waking once to her urging fingers and quickly extinguishing the fire inside her. Later he awoke in the darkness to the smell of wood smoke, and could see her bent over working hard at her fireplace. Where was her man? Eating bad food and rooting with bad women, he'd bet.

Carlos was already saddling the horses when Slocum went out with a candle lamp. The youth looked back at the jacal. "I could stay here forever with her."

"She is a lovely woman and a good cook."

"Should I ask her if she needs help when my job for you is over?"

"Sure."

The youth nodded in the coolness of the night. "I'll do that."

They'd finished packing and saddling when she called them inside for breakfast. They sat down for fresh-made flour tortillas wrapped around spicy beans and her goat cheese.

"Carlos wonders if you need a helper around here when his job for me is over."

She blinked. "All I could do was feed him. I make little money."

"What do you think?" he asked the boy.

"For your wonderful food and company, I would work for that," he said, smiling pleased.

She looked up and nodded at Carlos in the flickering orange candlelight. "I will look for your return."

"*Gracias, señora.*"

They rode out under the stars. Each wrapped in a blanket, they pushed their horses. Slocum wanted to end this odyssey and recover the woman. At midday, they took a breather. But there was no water, nor had they come across any. With canteen water and cloths, they washed the muzzles of their horses. Chewing on jerky, they mounted and rode on.

That night when the sun set, all signs indicated that they were close to the kidnappers. Slocum had never been through the country by this route, and neither had the boy, so they were hoping they'd find water. At sundown, dropping off the caprock, they found a shallow stream to water their mounts and packhorse. When they were well watered, he put a feed bag with corn on each animal. He'd not dared to feed them until they had a good drink.

"Wonder why those three didn't camp here," he said to the boy as the day fled into twilight.

"No firewood. Not many cow chips even."

"You're right, pard. I wonder how far they went on." Slocum shook his head over his lack of success in catching them.

"They're not feeding their horses grain. There's nothing left out here to graze on. Their horses must be getting weak."

"How do you know that?"

"By breaking open the fresh horse apples I find."

"Good scouting. We'll ride on for a ways tonight and hope we don't stumble over their camp."

Carlos agreed, and when their ponies finished eating, they rode west in the gathering darkness. Slocum was tired enough to sleep for a week, but he wanted the gap between him and those he pursued closed down.

"Wait," Carlos said when they reached a high place. "I can smell mesquite smoke."

Slocum nodded and peered out in the pearly light. Only

a half-moon for light. "Let's take the horses back, hobble them, and scout this out on foot."

An hour later, hearing a horse nicker, he reached out and stopped Carlos. "We're close," he whispered. "Real close to them."

The boy agreed.

8

Toby dismounted heavily in front of the hitch rack with a clunk of his spurs, and stared at the moth-eaten old buffalo-hide door. This place was rough. He pulled his pants out of his crotch and stretched his stiff back muscles. So far, they'd been following the right tracks. Good thing that they didn't erase very fast in this land. Even better that those two boys could read them.

If Slocum and Juliana weren't here, he'd be pissed off. But where were they going? Only thing he could imagine was Fort Dodge, Kansas, which was north of here a hell-uva long ways. The rest of this country was Comanche/Kiowa/Cheyenne land. Not a good place for a man that liked his scalp.

Kelso was acting strange and holding back. There must be a reason for that. Toby shrugged it off and handed his reins to Polo. "I'll go in and look the place over. See if there's any sign of them here."

The pair agreed, and rode for the pens.

Toby lifted the hide and looked around the dark interior, letting his eyes adjust to the bad light.

"Howdy, stranger, welcome to Cally. Whiskey is four bits a shot. Horse overnight's two bits and meals the same."

"Pour me one," Toby said, hitching up his chaps and bel-lying up to the ornate wooden bar that had obviously come from some grander place than this. "What's this Cally busi-ness?"

"We, sir," the whiskered big man behind the bar began, "have seceded from the Union. Since we receive no U.S. mail here despite my pleas with Washington, we have no law enforcement provided, except my sawed-off shotgun, or road crew to smooth out the ruts, we have decided to raise our own flag and call this Cally."

Toby frowned. "I'm looking for a man named Slocum. They say he has a woman with him that may be kin to me."

Woodberry nodded. "You're several days too late. She left with some outlaws and he left the next day."

After taking a quick swallow of his whiskey, he looked hard at the man. "Say that again?" He nodded for the man to refill the shot glass. "She left with outlaws?"

"They conked Slocum on the head and took her, I should have said."

"Who in the hell are they?"

"Three men drifted in here and drifted out with the lady."

"Slocum went after them?"

"Three days ago." Woodberry refilled his shot glass and recorked the bottle.

"Hell, they could be to Santa Fe by now. You holding any grudges against a trader named Kelso?"

"He out there?" Woodberry made a face like a man who'd smelled sour milk.

"Yeah."

"Tell him come inside. I won't eat him."

"I'll do that." Toby downed his whiskey and slapped two quarters on the bar.

He went over, lifted the hide door aside, and used his other arm to wave the trader inside. "He's forgiven you. Get in here."

With a shake of his head, Toby went back for another drink. Who in the hell where these men that Woodberry called outlaws? And why did they take her? Sumbitch.

They took her for their own piece of ass. No way they could know she was a discard. If she wasn't talking, they didn't know her from goat shit. But how was he going to get to her?

"Did Slocum go after them?" he asked, and turned to see Kelso entering the hide door. "Get in here. I'm buying the drinks."

"Well, where've you been?" Woodberry asked Kelso, looking him over.

"Trading's all I do."

Woodberry shook his head in disgust and set another shot glass on the bar. "You buying for him, too?" he asked Toby.

"I swear, Woodberry, I ever get the money I'll pay you," said Kelso. "I've had a tough run on bad luck. He asked you about that woman? I had her and I'd've gotten enough reward for delivering her to pay you what I owe you and more. That damn Slocum got her away from me and I couldn't chase him. He's a killer and—"

"Shut up. The man's buying you a drink." Woodberry gave him a scowl and pushed the filled shot glass closer.

"Ah, ah, sure."

"Who's got her? I mean what's their names?" Toby asked.

"Freckles, Rudy, and Earl."

"Who are they?" Tony turned to Kelso. "You know them?"

Holding the half-full shot glass, he shook his head at Toby. "Never heard of them."

"The story goes that they robbed some fella up in Kansas of lots of cattle sales money," said Woodberry. "They figured or knew that he'd sic the Pinkertons on them. So they were riding hard west."

Shit. Toby downed his third shot. That was all he needed. Someone else messing up his business. Now he no doubt had two groups to fight with over her. This gritty business of sleeping on the cold ground wasn't worth a damn. He'd eaten enough bad camp food to last his upset bowels for a long time. Plus he didn't trust Kelso. Nothing he could put his finger on, but Kelso wasn't telling him everything about

Juliana and how he came to be holding her. It wasn't the fact he'd been screwing her that bothered him either—he'd shut the door on her forever when those hired guns of his had hauled her ass off.

Such a perfect plan and now—now it had gone sour. He could think of twenty other things he'd rather have been doing than standing in this dark stinking saloon drinking sorry, high-priced whiskey with two smelly old farts. They acted like a couple of old tomcats ready to claw each other's balls off and could barely stand each other's company.

No women in this place, and if there were, they'd be so eaten up with venereal diseases that he wouldn't touch them. Worse than anything else, he needed to get this damn thing over with and get back to being a ranch owner. Not someone's flunky or day laborer. He'd worked all kinds of jobs before he married Juliana. All kinds. Like moving that hay for Old Man Pitch or cleaning outhouse pits for old ladies in town—he'd had all those bad jobs, but when he took over the 345, he'd moved into the kind of life he wanted to live. Let the help handle it. But this was his mess to straighten out, and he had to be certain he didn't screw up. This was where great plans had led to—a dead end.

"No idea where they went—these outlaws that took her?"

"New Mexico, I guess. You going to help Slocum get her back?" Woodberry asked him.

"Sure, soon as we can catch him," Toby replied, after seeing what side Woodberry was on.

"Horse feed is two bits a head. Hay's expensive hauled out here."

Toby nodded and paid the man. Then he looked at Kelso. "Come on, the boys'll have food ready."

Outside in the late afternoon wind, Kelso hugged his arms. "What the fuck did you mean back there—help Slocum?"

"Stupid, couldn't you see and hear he liked Slocum and didn't like the outlaws? Why not agree and be on his side?"

"Never thought of it that way." Kelso squeezed shut his right fist. "Wish I had Slocum's balls in my grip. I'd smash them to pieces and then squeeze them apart between my fingers. That sumbitch is the cause of all this."

"We can ride hard enough, we may catch him."

"I want him."

"We're leaving before dawn. I want him, too. You said she didn't talk when you had her. Didn't or couldn't talk?"

"She didn't say a word. You could wave your hand in her face and she would look right through it."

"Lost her mind, huh?"

"I guess. She sure wanted to run away from me, and hell, I was saving her ass from them horny red savages. Couldn't figure it."

"Why do you think she wanted to run away from you?"

"Damned if I know."

"I guess we'll only know when we get her."

"Sure. Sure. But I've got a bad feeling about this deal."

Toby didn't give a gawdamn about Kelso's feelings. "Where we headed next?"

"There's a woman west of here. She's got the only water until the Devil's Fork River, which is a good day's ride past her place."

"What's her name?"

"Dominga."

They were up at dawn. Kelso cussed and belly-kicked his honking mules while loading them. They soon were ready to sail. Toby rode out with his two men, and it was near noontime when Kelso, who had been trailing them a quarter mile behind with his noisy mules, came busting his ass to catch up.

"Wait! Wait!"

What the hell was wrong now? Toby stopped his horse and scowled at the trader as he reined up his spotted mule in a sliding stop.

"We've got big troubles. There's a war party trailing us back there and there's plenty of them."

"I thought Injuns didn't raid until their horses had grass

to eat. There ain't no grass out here. If we weren't graining our horses, they'd've starved to death by now."

"I don't care. There's twenty or more bucks on our ass right now." Kelso looked fidgety, glancing back over his shoulder like he wanted to get out of there and had nowhere to go.

"Who are they?" Tony asked.

"Comanche, I figure. They may think we shot them young bucks that Slocum killed."

"I thought you traded with 'em."

"These are some of them red bastards that only the Comancheros trade with. Not me."

Toby pulled the field glasses out of his saddlebags and focused on the country behind them. There were plenty of war-painted Injuns coming. Some had Henry repeaters; their brass actions shone in the sun. But having a repeating rifle and knowing how to shoot it accurately were two different things.

"Find us a place," he said to his pistoleros. "Where we can defend ourselves and our animals. Then limber your rifles. We may have hell popping around here any minute." The two boys looked around, and chose a place on the slope above them so the Indians had to come uphill toward them.

Toby agreed, and told them to get up there and to hobble the stock.

"How-how many you seeing?" Kelso asked, pushing in closer to Toby.

"Maybe twenty."

"Let me look. I may know them."

Toby handed them the glasses. "Well?"

"Black Horse." Kelso shook his head, "He's a real mean sumbitch."

"You screw his woman? Or him on some trade?"

"No, he's just bad mean."

"I don't like fighting your wars, Kelso."

"I don't like it either." He handed the field glasses back and spurred his mule and train for where the boys were already hobbling the other animals. Toby was right on their heels, wondering how well they'd stand up against the onslaught of two dozen bucks.

This wouldn't be any Sunday school picnic. Damn, more problems in his struggle to become a prosperous rancher. He would survive this day. He had to.

Screaming sonsabitches! They charged in riding half hung over the far side of their ponies. "Shoot their gawdamn horses," Toby shouted at his men.

The acrid stink of the black powder stung his nose and half blinded him. Through blurry vision, he made his Spencer bullets count. A piebald horse went nose-down, sending its rider flying off into the mesquite brush. Next round, a screaming buck threw up his arms, hit square in the chest with a .50-caliber slug

They began taking a toll on Comanche horse stock, and caused enough wrecks that the circling Indians rode off to count losses. Polo's arm was bleeding from a bullet fragment, they decided. Guerra bandaged him when the shooting let up. Kelso had two scratches from shots by the raiders.

"What are them red fuckers going to do next?" Kelso asked, using some whiskey on his scratches.

"How should *we* know? You trade with 'em."

"Not that bunch out there. Them's the bad ones."

Toby didn't like the looks of things. Those bastards were coming back for more. Hell, they'd lost a half dozen bucks and maybe that many horses. But they came charging in again.

Taking deadly aim, Toby shot, piled up a big roan horse in the lead, and two more flipped over him. Their riders scrambled for cover. Bullets whizzed by his head. Then one struck him. Hard in the chest. He couldn't catch himself and fell backward.

"You all right?" Kelso shouted at him.

Out of wind, he couldn't answer, and waved Kelso back to shooting so the bucks didn't overrun them. He held his hand to his wound and then looked at the blood. Holy crap, he was going to die out in this godforsaken land looking for a damn woman who should have been dead.

Gun smoke, Indians screaming, the confusion of their own horses stomping around, some horses hit by the bullets—he lay on his back with a burning wound in his chest, and was barely able to do little more than sit up and empty his handgun at the charging Comanche.

In the next charge, Toby fell backward, clicking his empty six-gun, and at last, in deep pain, he fainted away.

9

With the three outlaws sound asleep, Slocum figured he might have a chance of getting her out of their camp. He and the boy were sitting on their haunches not fifty feet from the snoring outlaws. It would be easy enough to shoot all of them as they slept—that wasn't his way. He simply wanted her out of there, and they could jack off the rest of their lives for all he cared.

Moving quietly around the circle of bedrolls with the stinging smoke from the campfire coals burning his eyes, at last he found her under a blanket with her hands and feet bound. At his shake of her shoulder, she awoke acting disoriented, saw him, and started to sit up. With his skinning knife, he cut her loose, and she scrambled to her feet. He put his finger to her mouth to indicate she should move quietly. Then on tiptoe, he led her by the hand out of the camp under the stars.

Carlos had cut all the lead ropes or untied the halters on the outlaws' horses, except for the extra horse taken for her to ride. They quietly herded the rest ahead of their flight. Slocum noticed that she limped some.

Concerned about her condition, he waved the boy over,

and then he loaded her on the extra horse. Then they let the loose horses go.

"Let's get the hell out of here," Slocum said in a low voice to the boy.

Carlos agreed, and they began to run for their own animals in the starlight with the woman on the stolen horse that they were now leading.

When at last they reached their mounts, and began chousing the packhorses, Slocum could hear the outlaws cussing in the night. Good, you walk home, wherever in the hell that is. In the saddle, he gave a nod to Carlos to take the packhorses on. He'd follow leading the woman's mount. Seeing her shivering in the starlight, he rode in close and put his blanket over her shoulders. She clutched it shut without so much as recognizing him. But he realized that she knew the difference between him and those other three.

They rode northward most of the night. He took this route simply to escape the gang, and by daylight they were at a small stream where they watered their horses. Carlos found enough dry chips to make a fire, and boiled them some of his special oatmeal and raisins. Slocum was about starved, and grateful there were plenty of cooked oats for a second round. She apparently was hungry, too.

When they finished eating, she unceremoniously rose, undressed like no one was around but her, and waded out in to the shallow water. Using handfuls of sand, she scrubbed herself in the stream.

"Don't look at her," Slocum said. "She's alone in her own mind to escape the bad things that have happened to her. Let her think we don't see her."

Carlos nodded, no doubt impressed by her beauty and the condition of her mind. "She is very pretty. But no one knows her name?"

"I don't, and that one-eyed whiskey trader didn't. At least he said he didn't. I'm not sure he told me the entire story about her. There were several Comanche bucks in the deal, and they came back after her, which I can't understand. I simply don't know the whole story."

"Very strange," Carlos said.

"I'm not certain that they can't catch their horses and take up our trail. Maybe we should have shot them in their sleep."

The boy shook his head in disbelief. "You couldn't do that."

"If I was angry enough, I could. I was mad about how they treated her."

"Only a coward would kill them in their sleep."

"For a boy without much raising, you sound smart enough." His original plans had changed about staying there—they needed more distance between them and Earl's gang.

Carlos shrugged under his threadbare shirt. "I only see how people act."

"You've done well. She's dressed again. I'll put her on the horse. We can catch that sleep later." He looked to the southwest. There was a good chance those three had taken up their trail by this time, if they'd been able to round up their horses.

They trotted their ponies and moved northward. Although it was miles north, he had in his mind Fort Supply, the new fort being built for the army south of Fort Dodge, Kansas. It might be too far away. To the east there was Fort Concho. He could go there. He needed a place with some protection for her safety. Also, someplace to send out posters from to see if they could attract any relatives to come forth and claim her.

Someone knew who she was and who she belonged to, even if she herself didn't.

"Maybe we best head east to Fort Concho. Who knows what those three bastards will try to get her back."

Carlos nodded. "It is many days east, huh?"

"Yes, but there will be army protection for her there."

The youth mounted up as Slocum helped her up onto her horse's back, using both his hands as a stirrup. They were off again, and with not much of a plan in Slocum's mind except to move toward Fort Concho.

Late in the day, looking through his glasses, Slocum picked out some dust boiling up on their back trail.

"Damn. I think they're following us."

"What should we do now? We should have stolen their horses, or better yet, we should have shot them in their bed-rolls." Carlos looked upset.

At last, they both laughed.

"Just keep moving, I guess. Maybe something will turn up," said Slocum

In an hour, they found a wide swath where an entire tribe had passed earlier. The ground was plowed up by travois poles packing tents, camp supplies, blankets, and cookware. They fell in, using the torn-up ground as their road and hoping to confuse those three behind them. Then, when the ground turned hard, they cut east again, and hoped they had left no prints that Earl's bunch could read.

"How many Indians were in that bunch?" Carlos asked.

"It was a big camp. I have no idea."

Carlos nodded. "I lived with them once. But I never felt good there. Like they were not my people. I wanted to be with Americans. Indians had few things like kettles to cook in. Their camps stank and they were cruel."

"Cruel?"

"Yes. If a man fell off a horse, others laughed at him. Men beat their women with whips."

"There's cruel men all over this earth."

"There are too many cruel men in the Comanche camps."

"I don't blame you for leaving them."

"That is why I know you could never have shot them in their sleep. Because you are not cruel to me or her, and she is not any relative of yours, yet you care for her like she is."

"She came from somewhere that she belongs in like a key in a lock."

Carlos agreed.

Before the sunset, Slocum scanned their back trail again with his glasses. No dust. Perhaps they had shed their pursuers.

"Tonight we must take turns being guards."

Without water for their horses, they washed off the animals mouths with wet cloths. Then they picketed them since there was no graze. Slocum decided not to feed the animals any oats, since they had no drinking water and might colic.

The sun heated up the next day, and at mid-morning they found a shallow moon lake to water their mounts and let their bellies settle before feeding them. Seated on the ground, they let the horses stand hipshot and rest before they hung feed bags on them.

They chewed on peppery jerky. Carlos even napped some while they waited. When Slocum thought their stock would be all right, they fed them and later moved on. Soon, heat, alkali dust, and a general weariness set in on all of them. He knew they needed to find a good place to rest for a day, but that required water, shade, and grass. Night guard duties, the hot sun in the daytime all drained their energy. Even with no sign of pursuit, the pressure was there all the time. They were in Comanche land.

She slept with him, but only as a body. There was none of the fiery woman from before. He wondered about the change, but didn't push her. She'd had another bad experience with men. Besides, he was bone tired and found no relief in a few hours of troubled sleep. He also was concerned about the toll on their horses, which were existing on a few handfuls of oats.

That evening they found water and bunch grass. The grass was brown, but at least would separate their guts. Carlos had located the water hole by tracking down some mustangs that used it. During the night, the stallion that ruled over the small band of mares and colts stayed outside their camp and sounded loud challenges at the invaders of his territory.

At dawn, they rode on with a little life in their horses' gaits. Midday, they found an abandoned adobe house with a shingle roof, corrals, and a dug well. There was a faded sign tacked on the door written in pencil. I COULD NOT SELL THIS PLACE SO I MOVED BACK HOME TO HELL. HELP YOURSELF. CHARLIE GREEN

Slocum laughed about it as he drew up water for the ponies. This was the first decent drinking water he'd tasted in days. Carlos was rounding up chips to build a fire in the sheet-metal stove inside. The woman was standing beside the corral, looking off at some foothills in the south.

What made her so interested in them? Did she recognize some she knew? When the horses at last seemed full of water, Slocum went over and stood by her.

"Are you all right?"

No answer. Then she turned, clutched him, and began crying on his dust-covered vest.

"Girl, if I could I'd fly you on the back of an eagle to your home, I'd do it right now. But you have to talk to me."

He wanted to scream at her—*talk*—but it would do no good. He simply held her and rocked her back and forth, both of them standing toe-to-toe. The afternoon wind swept dust by them, but it did not matter. They were enclosed in time by themselves. This was the first time since he'd rescued her that she'd acted like she was attached to him.

What was going on in her head? Why couldn't she talk? He wanted to unlock so much while holding her slender, ripe body to his. Where was her husband? Dead in the attack where the Indians got her from? Or was he walking the floor somewhere, wondering where she might be—if she was dead or alive?

Then she caught his face and kissed him with all the power and strength of a normal woman anxious to entice him into having sex with her. Damn. Damn.

10

Toby had seen the raging anger in the face of the Indian who was riding by at breakneck speed, screaming like a madman, and firing his Henry. The Indian was the one who'd put the bullet in him. Lying on his back and wondering if they'd bury him, Toby began losing consciousness. Shots and screams of men and horses could be heard all around him. Toby worried that their own stock would stomp him to death as they danced about, some wounded. Then he fainted, and it was late in the day when he awoke. His chest felt like someone had driven a spear into him. It hurt like fire to cough. He listened. The only sound was the snort of their nearby horses. No shooting. No war cries.

"You awake?" Kelso asked, kneeling over him. "I got some whiskey for the pain. Can I hold your head up and you sip it?"

"Where are the fucking Indians?" Toby asked in such a rusty-sounding voice that it shocked him.

"Gone. We won."

"My boys?"

"Polo's arm is okay. Guerra is scouting the dead ones to be certain they're really dead, huh?"

"They left their dead?" It hurt like hell when Kelso lifted his head and gave him some whiskey from the tin cup.

Damn liquor tasted like peppery piss. Bad stuff to drink. It was old cheap whiskey, but he needed more of it to ease the pain. Damn, how bad could his condition get? He was loaded up with a bullet in his chest. What were his chances of surviving out there in God knows where? No one could answer that for him. No one knew a damn thing anyway.

"We're close to that woman's place. She's kind of a witch, but she might could help you out," said Kelso. "But she ain't a whore and she gets mad as hell if you accuse her or even act like she's one. Don't make her mad. We need to heal you up to go find your wife, and this woman has the only place we can do it out here. Savvy?"

After Toby agreed, Kelso put more liquor to his lips. Sipping it made Toby cough and he hurt worse. Oh, hell, maybe he'd die and it would all be over. He closed his eyes as he started to black out.

Toby awoke on a pallet under a roof. Where was he? Where were his shirt and vest? He had on his pants under the cover. He must be at the woman's place. Where was she? His chest really hurt like he was hugging a fireball. With his right hand, he felt bandages on his chest.

"So you are alive," she said.

All he could see were her brown ankles and sandals under the ruffled hem of her skirt. He tried to clear his throat—that hurt.

"Yes," he managed to get out.

"Do you want that bullet out or left in you?"

He could see she was of medium height for a Mexican woman. She hugged her pert-looking bustline with her arms folded. Nice figure despite her age—he guessed thirties—not some big-bellied slob. Not a raving beauty, but he'd screwed worse-looking ones. He must be going to live. He had sex on his mind. "What's best?" he asked.

She looked undecided. "I think take it out. It's lead and

foreign to your body. Your wound probably won't ever heal if you leave it in."

"You took them out before?"

"Yes."

"Is it deep?"

She shook her head. "I tested for it while you were out. It is in the muscles. But I must cauterize it when I am through."

"What in the hell is that?"

"I will fill the wound full of black powder and set it on fire to seal the blood vessels. It also will keep down any infection. An infection would kill you."

He tried to look up at her. "You a doctor?"

"I have been one here to many men who have been shot, and in Mexico to those who were wounded."

"My name's Toby—Job Toby."

"I am Dominga. Your men and Kelso went on to find the woman those outlaws have."

"I bet I don't have even a horse to ride."

She shook her head. "They had to leave some pack goods because they were short on horses. Several were shot or had to be shot."

"This outlaw Earl, is he tough?"

"A mean sumbitch. He raped me when they were here, and I will kill him if I ever see him again."

"This woman they have?"

"Oh, they have abused her so. I hope Slocum reaches her and cuts their balls out for what they have done to her. She doesn't answer anyone. She never spoke. Her eyes have a film over them. And she is so pretty. Is she kin to you?"

Toby nodded. "You need them here to operate on me?"

"No, but I must strap you down, because even full of laudanum, you will have pain."

"How can you do that?"

"A man a few years ago who I operated on to get some arrowheads out of his back, later made the straps for me as a present."

"Nice of him. You think Slocum will catch them?"

She nodded.

"He ever tell you why he had her?"

"No, but he is a good hombre."

"Others say he is a killer."

"Maybe he kills those who need to be killed."

Toby closed his eyes. "When you get ready, take the damn thing out. I have a ranch to run."

"I will have to boil my things and get you on the table."

He nodded and closed his heavy eyes. In seconds, he fell back asleep. A troubled sleep with dreams about Juliana. The night he handed her over to the two pistoleros, she was heavily doped on laudanum. He dreamed that she came back to the house naked. He had to gag and tie her up in the saddle room, then lock the door so the house help didn't see her. Then he and Valdez argued about those sorry bastards that his man had hired to take her away. They were arguing when one of the house girls, Tia, came in and told him that his wife was in the barn screaming. So to keep Tia quiet, he choked the girl to death with his bare hands so she didn't tell the others. He was busy killing the house help one by one to conceal his plan. Then he woke up screaming.

In front of his blurry vision, the woman held in her fingers the .50-caliber bullet. "I have it out. Lie still. I must stop the bleeding," she said, getting up off her knees to go for something.

Soaked in his own sweat, he found he was bound head to toe on the hard boards under his back by several thick leather straps. The urinelike smell of gunpowder hit his nose as she filled the wound. Then she threw a towel over his face.

There was a flash that came through the cloth, and at the lightning pain in his upper chest, he pissed in his pants. He could hear himself screaming, but it sounded so far away—then his world went black.

When he awoke, she was there on her knees beside him. "How are you today?"

"I don't know. How long have I been out of it?" He realized he had no clothes on under the light cover.

"A day. But that is good. You heal better asleep than fussing."

"Am I healing?"

"I can't tell this soon. But it shows no angry red signs of infection."

"I will owe you for saving my life. What do you want?"

"What can I have?"

"Money?"

"I would take money. I need some things. A pump for my well and more goats. The coyotes are hard on them. They eat more of them than I do."

"In late summer, I will have the money from a cattle drive and I will pay you with goats, a pump, and cash."

"Fine," she said. "I will help you up so you can use the toilet."

"I'm naked."

She laughed. "Who has changed your bedding and washed your pants and wiped your butt while you were out of it?"

"Sorry."

"They are normal things." She shrugged them off, pulling on his good arm. "Get up easy, you may faint. I can't hold you up."

He nodded, and she was right. His head did get very dizzy when he stood on his feet, and she took her time getting him outside into the too-bright sun. He emptied his bladder in the dirt beyond her door. The strong wind swept his bare skin until the last dribble came out. Then he nodded that he was ready to go back inside. Shuffling his bare soles on the hard ground and relying on her as a crutch, he headed for the open doorway.

How were his pistoleros doing? He didn't like the fact that the cowardly whiskey trader, Kelso, was leading them. Besides, what was Kelso's real intention here? Kelso might have sold her back to the savages if Slocum had not found her in his camp.

Before Dominga helped him to lie down on the pallet,

she laughed at him. "You must be getting better. Your friend down there is coming alive."

She meant his dick. Glancing down, he realized his rod was halfway stiff. "What can we do about that?"

She tapped him on the good shoulder with her small index finger. "You are too weak to do much more than lie on your back. I can handle the rest."

And she did so, with her hot mouth and fierce fist, until he emptied his balls in a great fountain on his belly. Then he fell unconscious and went to sleep.

The next day, his boys Polo and Guerra still had not returned, and he began to worry about them. They should have caught those bastards by this time and been back. Even if he was able to ride, he couldn't leave this place. He had no horse to ride.

Three more days passed, and he was pacing the jacal's hard-packed floor. She came in with her hands full of goat entrails from the billy she had just butchered.

"Your men are returning. They seem to have several horses with saddles and packs."

"Oh, thank God," he said. Hurrying to the doorway to greet them, he grew light-headed and sunk his shoulder against the door facing as he saw Polo and Guerra approaching on some fine horses.

"What took you so long?" He frowned at the two as they dismounted. "Where's Kelso?"

Polo looked around as if to be sure they were alone. The dirty bandage on his arm needed to be replaced. He waved Toby over to a dun packhorse. Toby took unsteady steps until he was standing beside it. He used the horse to steady his balance on. Looking serious, Polo undid the straps and lifted the flap for him to see inside the canvas pannier.

Bundles and bundles of money. More gawdamn U.S. paperbacks than he'd ever seen in his entire life. Thousands of dollars.

"Where is she at?" Toby asked.

In Spanish, Guerra, standing behind him, said, "Like the smoke, she is gone."

11

The abandoned ranch proved to be the best place for the three of them to rest. Carlos spent the days out on a high point using the field glasses, seated cross-legged on an old blanket under the lacy shade of a mesquite bush, looking for any signs of riders' dust.

They drew water and took baths in the horse tank. Slocum worked on the worn-out portion of their tack, repairing it and making certain it was sound.

She mended their clothing. Deep in her own world, she walked among them like they weren't there. She spent long hours under the canvas shade that Slocum hung up for her, looking off in the distance at something he couldn't see. She never even hummed. If she heard Slocum or the boy speak, she never answered or showed any sign that they were there. But when she and Slocum were alone or in the bedroll, she would make wild, fierce love to him. Completely unrestrained and driving hard—during the wildest part of the lovemaking, her vaginia contracted like a man's fist and grunting noises would come from her throat, but no words, not even when they came.

All at once, she would become as excited as a tornado and couldn't get enough of his dick, but when she finally let

go, she would sleep for hours in a stupor he couldn't wake
her from. There was never any expression on her lovely
tanned face—no smile even.

He'd swear she'd smiled a time or two in the beginning
after they'd had a good session in bed, but that was before
the outlaws took her. That experience must have pushed her
over the last cliff. One night, they were having supper—
rice, frijoles, bacon, and corn bread—when she rose on her
knees, put down her plate, and then came over to kiss him.

Slocum knew what she wanted. He said, "Carlos, let us
be alone."

"I'm leaving. I'm leaving." The youth scrambled to his
feet and ran outside, trying to suppress his laughter.

She had him on his back and was rubbing his crotch.

"Hey, Slocum," Carlos shouted. "You better get out here.
We've got company coming. Bring your rifle, too. It ain't
nice company either."

He set her hands aside, holding both her forearms, and
shook his head. "Not now. We have company."

Her eyes welled with tears, and she fell on the pallet si-
lently crying. Nothing he could do about her for the moment. He jerked on his boots and hopped across the room,
pulling the last one on. He straightened up in the doorway
to see four single-feather bucks on horseback by the corral.
The sun's last rays gilded them in the golden light. On their
chests they wore eagle bone breast coverings and balanced
rifle butts on their bare brown legs while holding back their
calico ponies, which seemed to be pawing for a drink.

Slocum shifted his rifle to his left hand, and held his
right hand up in a peace sign, while looking the Indians
over closely for any sign of aggression about to spring up.
They looked safe enough for the moment.

One rode forward. In sign language, he said his name was
Red Hawk. They and their horses needed a drink. It had been
a long ride for them. Would he allow them to get water?

He motioned for Red Hawk to sit down, and called Carlos over to translate.

"Tell the others to come also," he said to the boy.

When Carlos spoke, they nodded and bailed off their horses. Adjusting their loincloths, they looked around suspiciously, then joined Slocum and Red Hawk in a half circle seated on the ground.

"Tell then I must know about a white woman that was among them."

Carlos spoke with little hesitation, and they searched each other's faces as if they were unsure they should tell him anything.

"Tell them it's the woman who has no tongue."

They began to nod and talk about a whiskey trader getting some men drunk and taking her from them.

"Where did they find her in the first place?" Slocum asked.

When Carlos translated their words, Slocum frowned. "They say two Mexican pistoleros traded her to some Comanche bucks for four horses."

"Who were these men?"

"They say that those men brought her doped, tied, wrapped in a blanket, and belly-down over a horse. They said to kill her if she ever tried to escape, for if the white soldiers learned that they had fucked her, they would cut off the manhood of every buck they caught. Even dead, they would need their manhood in the next world."

"That's why they were after her." Slocum sat with his Spencer over his lap. "All we need to know is how those Mexicans first got hold of her and where that was so we can take her home."

"Should I tell them she is with us?" Carlos asked.

"Tell them we can fix it with the army so the soldiers won't harm their body parts either dead or alive."

When the boy finished telling them that, Red Hawk stuck out his hand and they shook on it.

"You'll be safe leaving his land, he says," Carlos explained.

"That's good. Ask him where those Mexicans were from."

Carlos came back with: "From the direction of the Llano River."

"Good. Someone back there will know who she is then."

Carlos looked at the ground as if troubled. "What will they do with her?"

"Put her in a home, I'd guess. Maybe in time, she'll come to her senses."

"That would be a big shame, wouldn't it?"

"What are you thinking?"

"We could keep her in Cally. Nobody would mind her ways there, that's for sure. Me and Woodberry would look after her. She could be free anyway. What do you think?"

"If I think her family can't take care of her, we'll do that. I thought you might go back to Dominga when all this was settled."

"Oh, she don't need me as bad as maybe this lady does. What if we leave her at Cally and go look for her people? Then they won't know she even exists until we tell them when and if the time comes."

"What are you thinking really?"

"I've been an outcast myself among the Comanche and white people, too. I know how bitter it is—"

Slocum stopped him. "Tell Red Hawk to water his horses and may the spirits of the wind and the great eagle ride with him."

They all rose, making head and hand motions that they were grateful, and the bucks went to water their horses. When Slocum and Carlos drew close to the house, the woman came to the doorway and handed Slocum his plate of food.

"Have we got enough left to feed the Indians, too?" he asked Carlos.

He nodded and went over to tell the Indians there was food for them. At the news, each of the bucks smiled and waved at Slocum.

With his back to the wall and picking through his food with a fork, he tried to piece together the entire story as he knew it. Two Mexicans had brought her to the Comanches under the influence of drugs, and traded her for four horses. How much were four horses worth? Very little. Why would two tough border pistoleros risk their lives trading a pretty woman for some worthless horses?

Why, she'd bring no less than five hundred in gold from the Mexico white slave trades. Those ponies wouldn't clear a hundred dollars in this country. Besides, most folks were broke from the recent war and there was no money in Texas.

How did the pistoleros get her? He had questions galore and no answers, except that maybe she came from the western hill country. Should he do as Carlos asked, go there and ask questions before he delivered her? She might be much better off up at Fort Concho than with her own. He'd sleep on it.

A smile crossed his mouth as he chewed on his supper, standing outside the cabin in the growing darkness, four bucks close by eating with him and talking in their guttural language. Maybe he'd even sleep on top of her tonight. Oh, hell, this was a mess.

And there looked like there was no quick end to the situation he found himself in. In two days they could be at Fort Concho, in four more they'd be on the Llano River talking to folks. Maybe they could cut off some of that time, but they'd better get moving at sunup.

The big question was, could he trust these bucks not to steal his horses and gear? Best if he and the boy took shifts as guards to be sure they didn't do that.

So he let Carlos have the first shift. Then he went inside and climbed in to the bedroll to join her. When he threw his arm over her bare hip, she rolled over and began kissing him. In minutes, he was on top of her and they were riding for the end of the world. Raised up on his stiff arms over her, he felt the contractions inside her pulling at him like a whirlpool. Then she threw her head back and strained. The hot flush from her went all over his privates and she fainted away. It was over for the night.

What would they do with her? A man couldn't have an

incoherent wife that dragged him off to bed whenever she wanted to have sex with him. Why, such actions would shock society. He chuckled to himself and reached over to gently fondle her long teardrop breast.

12

He was hardly able to contain his own excitement. Where did all this damn money come from? Didn't someone say Earl Simpson's gang had held up a cattleman in Kansas and the man had put Pinkerton on their asses? Hell, with this much money, he could buy the whole damn hill country— he didn't need Beth Ann's family or her cold hatchet ass any longer. He was filthy rich. Now, all he needed was his wife planted out there somewhere, and he could ride back to the 345 and really start living.

"Was she there?" he asked Polo.

He shook his head and looked around, then motioned that Dominga was coming.

"So you caught them?" she asked.

Polo shook his head. "She was not there."

"So Slocum got her, huh?"

Polo nodded.

"Well, he'll take her home. You don't need to worry. He's a good man, I tell you."

"Yes, yes," said Toby. "Fix them some food. They are very hungry."

"Oh, sure. We'll have some goat in a short while. I'll let you men talk."

"Thanks, Dominga." He still needed her. Watching her hips swing as she sashayed off, he thought about the fiery ass under the skirt. He needed her all right.

When he was satisfied that she was in the house cooking, he turned to his men. "Where did Slocum take her?"

"They did not know, Señor. We had that freckled-faced boy's balls in a wooden vise, and he told us they lost their tracks up north where an Indian village had moved by with travois and many horses. We crushed his *huevos* flat as a pancake, and he still told us the same story."

"That old man," Guerra said. "We did the same to him, and he said the same thing. I think this Slocum got her back and lit out."

"Think. All this money is no good without her. You savvy? Where's Kelso?"

"He rode off before we raided the camp," Polo said. "He never said a word. That sumbitch is loco."

"He know about the money?"

"No."

"Where was Earl when you were torturing them other two?"

They turned up their pale, calloused palms. Guerra said, "He vamoosed and was long gone. We looked all over, but could not find him. I don't think he left on horseback."

"How could he hide out there?" That sumbitch Earl had to have been around that camp. But his men had still done good.

"We wondered the same thing. But we never could find any tracks or anything. We were also worried there were some bucks in that area, and when Earl didn't show up, we loaded and rode back here," Polo said.

"Wonder where Kelso went."

His men shook their heads. Obviously, they had no idea. Both Earl and Kelso needed to have their throats cut and be left for buzzard bait. He still had lots to do. But his number-one problem was to find Slocum and Juliana. She was the one who could point the finger at him. But even she couldn't stop him now. With the outlaws' large take, he could go to

Mexico and live like a king. Still, he'd rather do that in Texas hill country.

How hard could it be to find a woman and three men? Juliana, Slocum, Earl, and Kelso. They'd find 'em. Maybe head for Woodberry's fort. It was the only place to get a drink, rest their animals, and try to learn where those four might be. Kelso would steer clear of there since he owed the man for something. But Slocum and Earl, if he was alive, could well be there.

They had to fix some shoes on the outlaws' packhorses. They were worn, but could be reset and would do for their trip back. Those lazy outlaw bastards hadn't done a thing for their horses. One was even minus a shoe, but there were some used ones in their gear that would work.

Dominga served them roasted goat, frijoles, and fresh tortillas. The two men nodded their approval at her food as they ate hearty. She sat and sipped a fresh cup of the coffee they brought her, a luxury she did not have. Toby wondered why such a woman lived way out here with her goats. She wasn't ugly and she had a nice little body. Made love like a mink—there must be a reason why she existed so far out in the middle of Comanche territory.

"Tell me why you live out here," he said.

"This is my place. I own no other land. This I have homestead papers for. I could not sell it to anyone and get enough money to buy a ranch, maybe near some town. All my life I say, 'Dominga you must own land so they can't root you out, huh?'"

He nodded. "Who built the jacal?"

"Randolph."

"Who was he?"

"A man I met a long time ago. He was a teacher. He read books. I called him my husband, and I always tell people he is in Mexico on business and will come back."

"How long has he been gone?"

She looked off in to the darkness. "Many seasons. So I suspect he is dead."

"Why don't the Comanche come and rape you and kill you like they do everyone else?"

She half smiled. "They have a chief—I cannot pronounce his name, but it is like 'ride with the wind.' He was shot and they brought him here. I fixed his wounds. He told me I could stay here forever and no one would bother me."

Toby nodded. "So you are under their protection."

"Something like that."

"I guess Randolph fixed the papers for you on the place?"

"Yes, he was so smart."

"Do you miss him?"

"Nights when the coyotes cry for their mates, I want to join them." Then she smiled.

"He teach you to be a doctor?"

She nodded, and then finished her coffee. "He knew many things and knew them well, too."

"I have a large ranch. I know what it is to own land and not to own land. My people were poor and we scratched a living out of dry land for other men."

"Then you know why I am here. People buy my water, and some food, and I have my goats, a few sheep, and chickens. I card my wool and make blankets."

"You liked this Slocum?"

She turned her head to the side. "He is a man any woman would like." Then she snapped her fingers. "Just like that."

"He say where he came from?"

"He came from Woodberry's fort, I think."

That was no help. He stole Juliana from Kelso, or so that lying galoot said. Hell's fire, when they got those horses shod, they'd do some hard riding. That night, he shared her pallet, and used her body hard, trying to forget about the bad things he faced. His efforts on top of her only helped for a short while, and within seconds after he came deep inside her, he began to fret about where Slocum and Juliana were.

The following morning, he generously paid her forty dollars from the loot for her doctoring. She had no idea about his secret stash of the money. He would have paid her more, but that might draw suspicion, since money in that part of Texas was so scarce. She jumped up and hugged his neck. His sore shoulder complained, but he enjoyed her attention.

She whispered in his ear, "They crushed that freckled sumbitch's nuts?"

"You heard? Yeah, mashed them flat in a vise they made from some small boards before they cut his throat."

"He deserved that. Tell them *gracias* when you are down the road."

"I will, Dominga. *Gracias* to you."

They rode two days and half of another night to reach Cally. They arrived past midnight, and seeing no strange horses or anything suspicious, they made camp, taking over an empty jacal.

A rooster woke him, but it was full daylight when Toby opened his eyes, and then he wandered over to the saloon-store. Four Indians, wrapped in blankets, sat outside on the ground with their backs to the adobe wall. Their brown eyes never flickered when he walked by them, lifted the buffalo hide, and ducked to go inside.

"I owe you for last night," he told Woodberry, who stood behind the bar. "You seen Slocum?"

"Came by here headed east."

"How long ago?"

"Couple days."

"He had the woman, huh?"

"He had some woman."

"He ever figure out who she was?"

"You want a drink?"

"Sure, whiskey. Did he ever learn her name?"

"Never said. Here's a glass." Woodberry poured him a double shot.

Toby downed half the whiskey, then set the glass down. "Not bad stuff."

"Ain't good either, but it's the best I've got. You seen that worthless Kelso?"

"Not in days and I don't miss him. I thought he might be here."

"He ain't been here. He owes me fifty bucks, and I may skin him for my money if I catch him."

"Where did Slocum go to?"

"East or south, I reckon. Never said."

Toby shoved the glass over at him. "I may need another." Why was Woodberry acting so tight-lipped about Slocum? Did he know the woman was Toby's wife? He'd better learn some more.

"Who was with Slocum when he rode out?"

"A boy works for me. And that woman."

"Did he ever find out who she was?"

"If he did, he never told *me*."

Toby shook his head to dismiss the subject before he got into it any deeper. Woodberry was no damn fool. He might have figured out something or Kelso had told him about her. Damn, everyone had became a suspect who could possibly expose him.

He finished his second shot. "What else I owe you besides horse feed and lodging?"

"I want to know why you, Kelso, and Slocum all have an interest in this woman?"

"I simply thought she might be a neighbor's woman that was taken captive."

"Then you had a name for her?"

"I talked to them outlaws after Slocum got her away from them. They said she came from Fort Worth."

Woodberry nodded. "So it wasn't a woman that you knew, huh?"

"No. I didn't know any woman from Fort Worth."

"Two whiskeys, a dollar, and how many horses?"

"Say a dozen."

"I'd settle for four dollars."

"Take five. Thanks for everything."

Toby and his outfit rode out in an hour, headed southeast. A hundred yards out, Toby twisted in the saddle and looked back at the flag flapping in the wind. He should have killed Woodberry so he couldn't talk at all. Woodberry could count, and he might have noticed how they'd gained some horses that had once belonged to those outlaws. Damn, he hadn't thought of that. Never mind. It was not likely Woodberry would come around Mason and tell anyone.

He better find Slocum and finish the damn job so he could enjoy all this money.

There must be a hundred thousand dollars on that horse. Thanks, Earl.

13

Fort Concho sat on the greasewood flats, the adobe building beyond the dust-swept parade grounds and under the flapping stars and stripes on an extra tall flagstaff. Slocum still wondered what Woodberry meant when he'd asked him about a man named Toby and two pistoleros who also had been there tossing out questions about a woman captive. This Toby knew Kelso real well, too.

Slocum dismounted in front of the military headquarters. He stepped over and lifted the woman off the horse. For a moment, he held her while she found her sea legs. Then he took her up on the porch and set her in a chair.

Carlos joined him after hitching the horses to the rack.

"You watch her that she doesn't wander away while I am inside."

The boy agreed, and squatted down beside her.

Slocum nodded to the armed guard and went inside to the orderly's desk.

"May I help you, sir?"

"I have a woman outside that I recovered from the Comanche."

"Yes, sir. What's her name?"

"I have no way of knowing. She can't or doesn't speak."

"Many are like that, but after a while in a safe setting, they get better and they begin to talk. I have several posters of women and children that were taken by the hostiles."

"I might check them over."

"I'll call Captain Lawson. He would like to interview her, I am certain." The noncom handed him the stack of posters.

"Thanks, Corporal. I'll look at these."

He found two women with a description and age that might fit, and looked up as the captain returned with the desk man. They introduced themselves and shook hands. When he glanced back at one of the sheets, he saw the name—Juliana Toby.

"Where is this lady you brought in that Corporal Shanks told me about?" asked the captain.

"I have her sitting on the front porch. She's in a very delicate state right now and I don't want to push her over the edge."

Lawson shook his head, then put on his hat. "Sad state of affairs. I know. We get them all the time here. Recovered captives. They usually have little or no mind left."

Slocum followed him outside, and Carlos stood up beside her when the two men emerged from the doorway.

"How are you today, ma'am?" the captain asked, nodding at the boy.

Nothing. She simply stared across the empty parade grounds.

"Which one fits her?"

"This one. Juliana Toby." Slocum showed him the poster.

"Why do you think it's her?"

"Her husband has been looking for her according to President Woodberry."

"President who?"

"President Woodberry of Cally."

"Oh, that old fool at the outpost. So her husband's been out there looking for her, huh? That was good."

"Yes. But I fear for the wrong reasons. She'll be fine right here for a moment or two. Carlos can watch her for now. Let's you and me talk inside."

Inside the captain's office, he gave Lawson the story the Comanche Red Hawk had told him. The officer closed his eyes and shook his head. "Why did those men deliver her to them?"

"I wondered the same thing. Not for four horses. She'd bring five hundred to a thousand in the white slave market in Mexico."

Lawson tented his fingers in front of his face and leaned back in his swivel chair with a creak. "Unless those men wanted her killed by Comanche."

"The Comanche were going to kill her after the threat the Mexicans made."

Lawson frowned and shook his head in disbelief. "I can't even find the Comanche, let alone castrate all of them."

"I assured the Comanche I met that that wouldn't happen. I'll take her down to the hill country and see what I can find out. But I'm not going to leave her until I'm certain that she's in safe hands. I'll also contact the local sheriff and put him in on it."

"We can take charge of her from here on."

Slocum shook his head. "No, I'd rather be certain myself that she's in safe hands."

The officer agreed. "You're a brave man, Slocum. I don't know this fella who's her husband, but he has some questions to answer."

"Yes, he does."

"She's sure a beautiful woman. I can't understand— well, there is no way to understand some people's minds anyway."

"Thanks. Carlos and I'll be taking Mrs. Toby home."

"I'll need to file a report on this incident. Would you be willing to wait for Corporal Shanks to write it up?"

"That's fine. We have time. But as you see, she can't answer your questions. And she may decide to take off in the middle of it all." That was the best way he knew to describe her free-spirited actions to the officer.

"I appreciate your concern. You've been through a lot, no doubt."

"Nothing at all, Captain, compared to what she's experienced."

They rode southeast for Mason, and stopped at a rancher's place to camp for the evening.

A thin sharp-featured woman came to the front door of the low-walled ranch house when they rode up. She looked them over with sharp eyes.

"What kin I do fur you all?"

"We need a place to camp for the night and water our horses. We can pay you," Slocum said.

"You can camp here for twenty-five cents. What's the matter with her?" The woman's eyes narrowed as she studied Mrs. Toby.

"She's been a hostage of the Indians," Slocum said, dismounting.

"Poor thing. Bless her heart, she's lost her ever-loving mind, ain't she?"

"For now," he said as Carlos gathered the leads and reins to water the horses.

"Oh, she won't ever be right. They've ruined her."

In no mood to argue with the woman, Slocum lifted Mrs. Toby off her horse and sent her with the boy and the horses.

"You her kin?" the woman asked.

He found the two bits in his vest pocket and paid her. "No. We just managed to find her."

"How long's she been up there with them savages?"

"Too long, I reckon." He removed his hat. "My name's Slocum. The boy's name is Carlos."

"I seed her somewheres before." The woman squeezed her chin. "You taking her home?"

Rather than explain, he nodded.

"Well." She waved her arm to the north. "You can camp past the big water tank. Be by yourselves down there."

Slocum thanked her and joined the others. They unloaded the horses. She sat on a canvas roll and watched them pile off their gear and saddles. Then Carlos built a fire and started supper.

A short man came walking down and shook Slocum's hand. "Charlie Wiggans's my name. Essie said you had a Comanche captive you were taking home."

"I'm Slocum, that's Carlos. The lady seated over there is the one she's talking about."

"You know her name?"

"We think so. She's not talking, but she answers to a poster we saw up at Fort Concho."

"Doesn't talk at all?" Wiggans looked pained in the day's fading sunlight.

"Has not said a word in a week getting here."

The rancher took off his hat and beat his leg with it. "Damn shame. She's a beautiful woman. Where's she hail from?"

"Mason, we think."

"What's her last name?"

"Toby."

"Don't ring a bell. I belong to the Texas Frontier Society and know several folks in that organization from down there. I don't know that one—wait, wait, I think the state court listed a Mrs. Toby as officially dead here recently."

"I'm not surprised," Slocum said. "And I suspect they intended for her to be just that. That's why I am delivering her to the sheriff in that county and not her family."

"You mean she was deliberately turned over to those savages?"

"She was doped, bound tight, and gagged when two men traded her to the Comanche for four sorry horses."

"Who told you that?"

"A subchief of the tribe, and they were told if she escaped them and got back, that the army would castrate every Indian they caught including the dead ones."

"My God, man, you learned all that out there?"

"There's lots to learn if you can listen."

"My, my, those are some of the worst things I can imagine. I'm sorry Essie charged you for tonight. You deserve a reward for all your work. Good luck." Wiggans left them, and the three of them ate their supper in the twilight.

At dawn, they rode out again. Slocum was anxious to talk to the law in Mason before bringing her into the town. So they set up camp that evening with a farmer named Hertz, and put up a shade for the next day when Carlos was to watch her while Slocum went on into Mason.

She was her usual impassive self, sitting and staring off like she wasn't with them. He told Carlos to keep his eye on her, so she didn't run off or do anything else that could harm her. Slocum left the next morning for Mason.

He short-lopped through the mesquite, cedar, and live oak on the narrow road for town. At the courthouse, he waited in the reception area awhile for the sheriff to come out of his office. A tall thin man in his forties, the lawman looked serious behind his large handlebar mustache.

"Hans Goldman. What can I do for you?"

"My name is Slocum. I've recovered a captive of the Indians and we need to talk about how she became one, 'cause it's not what you're thinking."

Goldman looked around the near-empty reception area. "Come back in my office."

He showed Slocum to a chair and settled in another behind his large desk. "Now, this captive?"

"I have reason to believe that she is Juliana Toby."

Goldman reared back and looked hard at Slocum. "You know that the Texas courts declared her legally dead a week or so ago?"

"A rancher we stayed with a night back told me the same thing. I can't help it. She is alive."

"Now what is her story?"

"She's not talking, but others are." Slocum went ahead and told the lawman all he knew, beginning with Red Hawk's version and up to her husband's presence in the country where she was found.

"She's not talking at all?" The sheriff looked upset.

"Not a word in a week or longer. I could say she was absent to everyone around her."

"My God. Who were those men that kidnapped her, do you think?"

"Tough hired guns, I'd say, because they put the fear in to the Comanche. I believe her husband had something to gain by her supposed death. Those Mexican toughs could have sold her in Mexico for a thousand. They only got four Indian horses for her."

Goldman twisted his mustache ends. "Damn. He moved in that Woolsey girl awfully fast for a man who was mourning the loss of his wife. Where's he at now? I wonder. You saw him out there, huh?"

"No, but him and two of his men were out there looking for her. He may be back home by now."

"Is she in a safe place right now?"

"Safe enough. A boy in his teens that works for me is guarding her on a nearby farm."

"Should a woman be with her?"

"No. She's not talking. She looks through you. If she even knows that you're there, you're lucky. The boy can handle her and be certain she's not hurt. She trusts him too."

"This is terrible. If this really happened."

"It happened all right. That Comanche had no reason to lie about her."

"I better ride out to Toby's ranch and see what he has to say about it."

"Mind if I tag along?"

"No. In fact, you might be the good help I'll need."

The man strapped a gun belt on his waist under his suit coat. Then he hung his head out the door to tell his clerk that he was going out to the 345 Ranch and talk to Job Toby. They left, and went to the livery to get Goldman's horse, a long-bodied Thoroughbred horse he called Midnight. When they rode out of town, their appearance came under the suspicious eyes of several bonnet-wearing women on the boardwalks.

"Be gossip all over now." Goldman chuckled. "Mason County sheriff and a stranger rode out of town together this morning. Something is up."

"You don't have much trouble here, do you?" Slocum asked.

"Not many things like this. A horse stolen once in a while. A Mexican or two get drunk and have a knife fight. I run down more chicken thieves than anything else. These German people are hard workers and honest. I have some white trash that I suspect are up to no good."

"What do you know about Job Toby?" Slocum asked, riding stirrup to stirrup with the man.

"He grew up around here. His folks farmed, I guess. He was a barefoot boy one day, a cowboy the next, and then he married Juliana shortly after her father was killed in a wagon wreck and he took over the 345 Ranch."

"No children?"

"No. She have any out there?"

"I don't think so." Slocum waved off a friendly collie that came down a driveway to bark at them. "When men get involved in deals like this, many times they have other shady deals on the side."

"I don't know of anything."

"Just thinking. Since that Comanche subchief told me that story about how they traded for her, I've had a million things run though my mind to explain it."

"I bet you have. Especially bringing her back here and wondering if you were putting her right back in harm's way."

"That's exactly it."

"I've run through things in my mind. He's a skirt chaser. Can't hardly cover his tracks having affairs with Mexican women and a few others. None ever complain, so I guess he doesn't hurt them. But he keeps pretty busy at that."

"Maybe we need to talk to some of them discreetly?"

"Have to be discreet. I wouldn't want a volcano to erupt around here, but yes, one of them may know more than I do about him."

"Sure. Do you have a place where we can hide Mrs. Toby if he isn't home today? She's very unpredictable. Does not talk, and may get up and take a bath in front of everyone. So it would have to be a strong person with an open mind. She doesn't need to be strapped down, but she will require looking after."

"I'm thinking. We can find someone."

"Good. I don't think a jail cell is the answer. She may come back to her senses, but I don't want her shoved aside and abused. Then she won't ever recover."

"What do you do when you aren't saving people?"

"A drifter."

Goldman nodded as if he knew all he wanted to know.

They reached the 345 Ranch and a young fresh-faced woman came to the door. "Oh, Sheriff Goldman. Is something wrong?"

"No, is your hus—I mean Job Toby. Is he at home?"

"No, not yet, but I expect him any day, sir. What do you need him for?"

"I simply need to talk to him. You think he'll be back soon?"

"Oh, yes, I expect him back very soon, Sheriff."

"I am Beth Ann Woolsey, his fiancée," she said to Slocum. "We will be getting married shortly, when he gets back. Now that the court has declared his poor wife as deceased."

"John Brown," Slocum said, tipping his hat to her and hoping he didn't shock Goldman too much by the name change.

"Nice to meet you, Mr. Brown. Will you two come inside? I'll have some tea or coffee made for you."

"No, thanks, we better get back," Goldman said. "Tell Job to come by and see me as soon as possible."

"I will. Be sure both of you come to our wedding, Sheriff."

"Yes, ma'am," he said, and they left her and the ranch.

"I used Brown back there," Slocum said to Goldman when they were out on the road, "because by now, he knows

I brought his wife out, and I don't want him running off because we were there today."

"Good idea, Brown. He is liable to run if he has anything to hide."

"My way of thinking. That poor girl back there is in for a big shock, but I couldn't break the news that Juliana wasn't dead and have her tell him and he takes a powder."

Slocum laughed out loud. "Damned if you do or don't."

"Exactly. I want to thank you for all you've done. This business might have been swept under the carpet, so to speak, if you hadn't found out about her delivery to the Comanche. It still stuns me that anyone could do such an evil thing as that to such a lovely woman."

"Amen." This whole business had ground to a stop for him, but he trusted Goldman. The man was a sincere, knowledgeable lawman. Some things had to be worked out, and maybe Juliana would be all right there in time.

Where was Toby anyway? Coming back or still searching for his wife?

They arrived in Mason at dark. After shaking hands and promising to get together in the morning, both men went their separate ways and Slocum rode back to his camp.

"How did your day go?" Carlos asked, coming away from the fire to help Slocum unsaddle.

"All right, except I'm starved. Toby wasn't back, or at least he wasn't home yet."

"I have frijoles cooked and ready."

"Good, I can use them. How was she today?"

"Fine. She looked for you, I think. I never saw her pace the camp like she did today. It's the first day you've been gone maybe. But I could see she was looking for you—not just walking aimlessly."

"That may be a good sign. I am hoping that Sheriff Goldman, who is a good man, will have a home for her soon."

Carlos nodded. "I hope they are kind to her. She has been through so much."

"They will treat her right, or I won't leave her with them."

Carlos poured hot water in a small pan for Slocum to wash his hands, and then went to ladling out his supper. The aroma of the mesquite-oak fire was strong. It was glowing orange in the darkness as he dried his hands and then took the tin plate with beans and a spoon.

"Thanks. You think she had some of her sense return today?"

Carlos poured him coffee in a cup and delivered it. "I certainly do."

"You don't think you just saw what you wanted to see in her?"

Squatted on his heels beside him, the youth looked reflectively at the fire. "No, I think its real. She didn't have that same blank face she's had all this time since her rescue from that gang."

"You know," Slocum said between spoonfuls of hot beans with the saliva flooding his mouth, "you see things you want in situations like this, but they don't really exist. We just want them to."

"You will see. You will see."

Using his spoon to make his point, Slocum said, "You're really a big help, and I know you'll find a place before I have to leave here."

Then Carlos frowned at him. "Why would you have to go away?"

"There's places where I'm wanted. It's complicated, but I know they'll come along looking for me and I'll need to move on."

"You show me those men—"

Slocum held his hands up to stop him. "No, I want no trouble. I'll simply ride on."

"Maybe I can go with you then?"

"We'll see. These are the greatest frijoles I ever ate."

"Good. Do we need to do guard duty tonight?"

"Not here. Not yet anyway."

"Good. There's more coffee. I'm taking my bedroll, my .30-caliber Colt, and going up there under the trees and sleep if you don't need me."

"Have a good night's sleep." Slocum cradled the warm tin cup in his hands. The night had cooled down more than usual. In the north, a coyote howled at the half-moon and a few crickets were slow to creak. Must be a breath of air from the north coming down.

He went to the dark wall tent and slipped inside. Her soft breathing told him she was fast asleep. That was fine with him. He'd had a long day riding with Goldman out to Toby's ranch and back.

Undressed, he carefully slipped under the covers and pulled them up to his chin. The heat from her body sought him. He smiled, then lying on his side, tossed an arm across her waist. His move was like pulling a bell rope in a school tower. She rolled over, pushed him on his back, and climbed on his chest. Dragging her firm breasts over him to get on top, and then breathing in his ear, she whispered, "You're back."

Oh, my God.

14

Toby wanted to be home. The three of them were short-loping in late afternoon between their split-rail fences that hemmed in the lane. Their horses were heaving from the long run, but he wanted to be home and learn all that had been happening while he was gone. Had that sumbitch Slocum showed up with her yet? That could really change his plans. If he didn't have the robbery money, it would be different—but since he possessed all that loot, there were plenty of options left, if he was careful and quickly fled if Slocum had delivered her by now.

"Look!" Polo shouted. "It is Valdez coming." He pointed toward the rider heading for them.

"Something's wrong." Toby reined up his horse to a halt. "What's happened, Valdez?"

"The sheriff was here today asking for you to go by and see him. I thought I better find and warn you." Valdez checked his impatient horse stepping around in a small circle.

"He say anything else?"

"No, but he had a big man named Brown with him. No one knew him."

"You sure his name was Brown?" Toby looked hard at his man.

"I am not sure of anything. What did you learn?" Valdez asked.

"That she's alive and some sumbitch named Slocum is bringing her in. I thought he might be taking her up to Fort Concho."

"No sign of her around here. He never brought her to Mason anyway so far. I have a guard posted there watching for her if she comes in."

"I think we better clear out everything in the house and head out of here."

"You taking Beth Ann?"

"Hell, no, you can have her. I'll be glad to be rid of her ass."

"Where will we go?"

"A new place, perhaps in Mexico."

"Hell, the damn Apaches have that country bare."

"Then we can go to Colorado. I don't care. We've got the money to do what we want to do."

Valdez frowned. "Really?"

"Rest easy, *mi amigo*. We have enough to do what we want to do."

"But how?"

"Don't worry about *dinero*. We will get the best horses and strip the place of anything of value. She may be coming home, but not to anything."

When Toby dismounted at the house, he found himself besieged with questions by his bride-to-be. "Oh, you are home. How wonderful. Do you know they have decreed her dead? When can we get married?"

She was yapping like a small dog at his heels, and he finally had enough. "Listen, I will only say this once. I am not going to marry you. Juliana is alive and coming home. Now go get packed and go home."

"You what? You said she was dead. You lied to me—"

"Shut up. You're lucky to be alive. I said load your things up and get your ass out of here right now."

"When my father gets—"

His jaw cramped as the anger in him rose. "You like your father, don't you?"

"Yes."

"Then if you want that old bastard to stay alive, don't sic him on me, 'cause I'll kill him, cut his dick off, and stuff it in his mouth."

"W-what, what if I'm carrying your son?" She rubbed her flat belly.

"Then you better hurry and marry Piper Jordan and tell him it was born early."

"Oh, I'll kill you!"

He caught her by her thin arm and jerked her up in his face. "Listen, you spoiled little bitch. I'm going to bust your bare ass with a paddle like a schoolteacher once did mine if you don't do as I say right now. Now load your things and be gone in an hour, or I'm going to do that to you. Understand?"

"Yes."

He left her crying in a dining room chair. What did he want the most? The roan stallion and the mares. He'd take them. This trip would require more than one packhorse. He better tell Maria to put in more food, too.

Next, he bundled up his shotguns and rifles. Might be a need for them later. Being pissed off didn't just mess up his mind where he couldn't think straight. It also made him nervous as a long-tailed tomcat in a room full of rockers. Actually, he felt so agitated, he was trembling inside.

One thing for certain, by dark he had to be gone from there. His men could move the stock and pack train—he simply needed to be out of sight and mind.

How did such a smoothly planned operation get so messed up? How had he failed at this business of getting rid of his wife? Juliana's father had been no problem to get rid of. He'd simply had a wagon wreck and died with a little help from Toby. Good enough.

Maybe this plan had been too complicated. Never mind that. He'd start all over on another plan. He had the resources on the packhorse. Damn, who was watching that sumbitch? In quick steps, he went outside in the too bright sun and saw the horse with its precious panniers standing unattended.

About to shout for his men, he saw Guerra come from behind the horse, shaking his pants like he'd been off pissing. "Where is Polo at?" Toby asked.

The man looked around to be certain they were alone, then in a loud whisper said, "He is fucking that new maid from Mexico."

"I don't care. One of you must be with that horse at all times. You savvy?"

"*Sí,* he and I have been—"

"I don't care what you do. Be sure one of you is with that damn horse."

"I will see to it."

"We leave in an hour, so be ready."

"*Sí, señor.* We have you a fresh horse to ride already."

"Good." He went back inside. Hearing Beth Ann hysterically crying, he strode though the dining room ignoring her. His gun collection was on his mind. He'd take them all with him, and make Valdez a list of the other things he wanted brought along. There was little time. If he'd only caught that damn Slocum in time and gotten rid of Juliana. There would have been no witnesses. Bad judgment on his part all the way along. He'd kill that Kelso, too, when he found him. If he'd just left her out there, she'd have died in a short time.

From the cabinet, he took the silver engraved shotgun and two sniper rifles with scopes. There might be a need for them where he was headed. And the old Walker Colt—the one that had once been worn years earlier by a captain in the Rangers. He didn't bother with the Spencer rifles.

Panic seized his lower intestines. He grew more anxious by the minute about his predicament, trying to think of what to do next each time he stumbled outside with another armload and trying to get his mind working.

Get the hell out and be fast.

In a half hour, Valdez had his list and the men were loading all the things Toby said he wanted to take along. Polo and Guerra, with five packhorses, were ready to ride with him, and he swung into the saddle.

"What will happen to the rest of us now?" Maria asked from the porch. Her brown eyes were wet with tears.

Toby rode in close, handed the woman five twenties. "This should tide you over until the new owners take over."

"Gracias, señor. Vaya con Dios," she said.

He turned the big bay called Thunder and left the yard with his two men. The tight muscles in his back began to loosen, but when he reached the last high point where he could look back and see the top of the ranch house it was as if an arrow had struck his heart. The poor farm boy's dream was evaporating as fast as a hard-on. Sumbitch.

His jaw was set so tight that his teeth hurt him. So did the still-healing wound in his chest. He booted his horse to go faster, turned away from his past life, and looked toward his new one wherever that would be.

15

"Talk to me, Juliana." Slocum lay belly-down and propped on his elbows beside her in the bedroll. Spears of the golden rays of dawn were dancing on the tent floor in a small shaft of light that came between the folds of the front flap.

"Why?" she asked in a smoky-sounding voice.

"'Cause I need to know many things. Did your husband have anything to do with your kidnapping?"

"All that is fuzzy now. I can't see it. One day, though, I overheard him say to his *segundo*, Valdez, *She needs to go. Make it look like Comanches got her.*" Lying on her back, she swept the hair from her face with her fingers. "One day in a lodge later on—with some stiff-dick buck bouncing on top of me—I recalled that. Why did Job put me there?"

She blinked her blue eyes and rolled over on her side to face him. "Why can I see and think now? Most of the rest comes as a wavy dream, like I wasn't in my own body. I was outside looking at this woman that I barely knew who was dancing her way around slowly. She couldn't talk. I wasn't her, so I couldn't talk for her."

"Maybe someone smart could tell you. All I know is the woman who danced slow and I made love, too."

She reached over and pulled him closer to kiss him.

"No, you made love to me. Not her. But I was afraid if I talked to you, then it would scare her away and I would lose you."

"Is this other woman gone today?"

"I'm not certain."

"You know you are going back into a world that will hardly accept you?"

"I don't care. What about him?"

"Toby?"

"Job Toby. Yes."

"He wasn't at home yesterday. The sheriff and I went out there. But I think he'll run once he knows that you're back."

"Why did he sell me? I was his wife. I gave him the ranch he always wanted."

"He has another woman living with him—Beth Ann Woolsey I think was her name. They were to be married when your death certificate was signed."

"Her father has a bigger ranch." She shook her head wearily. "Now I wonder about many things. Do you think he killed my father rather than the wreck in the wagon?"

"Juliana, I think the man was personally a very selfish, mean person."

She nodded, and then squeezed her throat with her hand. "It hurts to talk that much."

He smiled at her and scooted closer. Things might go easier for her now that she could talk. Entwined in each other's arms, and soon with their bodies connected, they made love.

Carlos had breakfast ready when they emerged. He poured coffee and looked at her and then him. "What's different?"

"She's found her voice."

"Oh, thank God. That is wonderful news. You're going to be all right now?"

She nodded.

"That solves lots of things for me." Carlos looked at the sky and waved at it.

Slocum laughed and blew on his coffee. "He's my right arm. Chief camp cook."

They all three laughed.

Over his meal, Slocum considered what they had to do next. Go into town and report the crime. Get a warrant sworn out for Toby's arrest. Install her at the ranch with some personal guards in place. Then he'd be free to ride on. Sounded easy, but it might not be.

So the three rode into Mason after leaving word with Mrs. Hertz at the house that they would pay her for another night's stay when they returned. Which apparently suited the hard-looking woman fine. Coming across the hill country of cedar and live oak, they saw that things were getting ready for spring. Earlier showers had the bluebonnets about to burst forth in seas of blue. Several black-suited men driving their farm wagons, either hauling in produce or coming home with feed and seed, stared hard at them in passing. No doubt wondering who they were.

At the courthouse, they dismounted, Slocum helping her down. She tried to smooth her clothing. Obviously, she had brushed her hair. But the much-worn skirt and blouse were not what she had been accustomed to wearing in town, and she acted upset.

To make her feel assured, he crowded in close and guided her toward the front door. Speaking under his breath, he said, "I should have bought you a new dress yesterday. There is still time before this day is over to do that, and there are, as you know, several dress shops in this town anxious to have you back as a customer."

She shook her head, seeming amazed by his words. "You're a darling. My friend was so glad that you rescued her from that camp of outlaws."

Was she slipping away again? He certainly hoped not as he guided her down the hall and into the sheriff's outer reception room. The sheriff's clerk stood up and told him to go right on in to the inner office.

"Come on, Carlos," he said as the youth hung back. "He needs your side of this, too."

"Good morning, Mrs. Toby." The sheriff scrambled from his chair.

"How are you, Sheriff Goldman?" she said.

He blinked, and then frowned. "You found your voice?"

"I can't talk long. But yes, it has returned for now."

"Sit down, ma'am. We'll try not to wear you out. Slocum thinks your husband sent you to those Comanche."

"He did."

"I know that you've had an awful experience with those people. But you didn't simply fall in their hands and blame him for it, did you?"

"It's all very fuzzy, but one day I overheard him say to his *segundo*, 'She needs to go. Make it look like Comanche got her.' Then I was in their lodge. I think I was doped by my husband and sold."

"I'm going out and arrest him."

"Thank you."

"You will be here to testify at the trial?"

"I will, sir."

"All right, I'm leaving right now to go arrest him."

Slocum nodded. "We need to get her some clothing, and then we're going to her ranch, too."

"What if he's not come in yet?" Goldman asked.

"We'll see that she's well guarded."

"Fine." Goldman smiled at her with a nod of approval.

"Let's go find some clothing for you to wear," Slocum said to Juliana.

"Yes, let's do that. Is Mrs. Draper still in business, Sheriff?" she asked.

"Yes, ma'am. She'll be glad to see you."

"Thanks. It's just down the block," she told Slocum and Carlos, and they went out the office door after her.

At the sight of her, Mrs. Draper clutched her own bosom. "That really you, my dear Juliana?"

"Yes, and I need a riding outfit. I may need more if my husband threw my clothes away." Then, as if she had considered the matter, she said, "Mine wouldn't fit *her* anyway."

"You are right, my dear."

Juliana made a sour face, then smiled. "That's a shame isn't it? That they wouldn't."

"Was he shocked to see you?"

"The only thing that he's going to see is Sheriff Goldman."

"Oh?"

"You will read all about it in the next *Mason Gazette*, I am certain. Now the dresses." She held her hand to her throat and coughed.

"Mrs. Draper. Please don't ask her any more questions. She's very tired," Slocum said.

"Oh, dear. And who are you, sir?"

"My name's Slocum, and I brought the lady back here."

"And this young boy?"

"He's no boy, and he's my assistant, Carlos."

"Well, she is very lucky to have both of you." She gathered up her hoop skirt and with an armful of clothing, she said, "We must go in back to try these on, my dear, and find one to fit you."

"We shall be right back," Juliana promised Slocum.

Slocum and Carlos went outside and squatted on the boardwalk. The day had warmed up as they whiled away the time she spent inside trying on outfits.

"Will Goldman catch her husband?" Carlos asked.

"I hope so. He needs to be behind bars."

Carlos made a face. "Who are those hombres across the street?"

"I'd say they were Pinkerton men. No one else west of the Brazos dresses as if they were in New York like that but his detectives."

"Who are they looking for?"

"Probably those kidnappers who we got Juliana from. Earl Simpson and his gang, who robbed some cattleman up in Kansas of all of his proceeds."

"Why would they be here? Those three were headed west."

"Damn, you're right. Last we knew, they were going west.

You don't reckon they came back here for her?" Slocum got to his feet, looking around for the Pinkerton men. "Where did those two dudes go?"

"I think in that saloon over there."

"All right." Slocum stuck his head in the door of the shop. "Juliana, you stay inside here. We'll be right back."

"I'm about dressed—all right, I'll stay here."

Slocum and Carlos crossed the street between two light wagons and entered Joe Shark's Saloon and Billiard Parlor. The clack of ivory balls on the velvet table was the first thing Slocum heard as he pushed his way inside. The two detectives, clad in green-striped suits, stood at the bar, drinking beer from large mugs.

"Howdy," Slocum said. "You two wouldn't be Pinkerton men, would you?"

"What do we look like?" the one with bushy eyebrows asked.

"In Mason, Texas?" Slocum asked, and then ordered two beers.

"Yeah, in Mason, Texas."

"Like two out-of-place suit salesmen. Who're you after?"

"You the law here?"

"No, but I may have information for you."

"We're looking for Earl Simpson."

"I'd guessed that much. My name's Slocum, he's Carlos."

"My name's Ingles," the bushy-eyebrowed one said. "He's Perdue."

"Good to meet ya. I heard somewhere that Simpson was on the run from the Pinkertons over the robbery of some Texas cattleman of his proceeds from a big drive."

The skinny one, Perdue, nodded. "You know where Simpson's at?"

"Last I knew, him and his partners were riding west for New Mexico," said Slocum.

"Well, his partners are dead now and whoever killed them crushed their balls before they died."

Slocum scowled at the man. "Crushed their balls? Where did this happen?"

"Out in the Llano Estacado over a week ago."

"Who did it?"

"We think a local here by the name of Toby may have ordered it done to them. He had two pistoleros riding with him that people say were very tough hombres."

"Who was killed?"

"A kid called Freckles and a rough old man called Rudy."

"Where's Earl?" Slocum asked.

"We think he came here after that man named Toby, who may now have the stolen money."

"The sheriff wants Toby. He's gone to arrest him."

"Good. He gets him, we'll take him back to Kansas for trial."

Carlos was through with his beer, and Slocum started to slap two dimes on the bar. Ingles stopped him. "We're buying the beer. Mister, you get any information on either of them, we'll see you get a big reward."

Slocum thanked the two men, and then he and Carlos left to go back across the street to the dress shop. He found Juliana inside wearing a divided tan canvas riding skirt, a long-sleeve brown shirt, and a flat-crown felt hat.

Slocum nodded in approval. "You look nice."

"I still need some boots."

"Where do we go find them?"

"Over at Pitch's in Decore. Can we ride over there next?"

"Let's go." He held the door open.

On the sidewalk, she caught his sleeve. "My husband owes that woman back there over three hundred dollars for dresses he bought for that hussy he's been living with. Can you imagine?"

"I figure that's probably not the only hump in the road. We spoke to Pinkerton men who are here looking for him who say he has the money taken by a gang up in Kansas from a cattle seller."

"How could I be so dumb?"

He clapped her on the shoulder. "You had no way to know."

"I sure didn't. Why, I may spend the rest of my life paying off his debts." She shook her head.

Two hours later, they found the sleepy village of Decore on Hurst Creek quiet, save for a few town dogs barking at them. Slocum dismounted in front of Pitch's Mercantile, and helped her off her horse.

She reset her new black hat on her head before entering the door he held open.

A shorter woman in her thirties, nice set of breasts, thicker-set than Juliana, greeted her. "Oh, my God, you are alive, Juliana."

They hugged.

"Why, let me look at you. You look wonderful."

"Margie, let me introduce the two men who saved me. This is Slocum and that's Carlos."

"Oh, how wonderful. You two are real heroes. My gosh, we should have a celebration."

"No. Margie, I need a pair of socks and boots."

"Sure. Does your husband know you're back?"

"No. The law has gone after him. He's the one who sold me to those red devils in the first place."

Margie threw her hand to her mouth, managed a short cry, before her face went snow white. Then her knees buckled. She fell to the floor unconscious.

16

Toby looked back over his shoulder as they climbed the trail single file through the live oak and cedars. Polo grinned at him and pushed his horse up closer.

"You need something, Señor?"

"No, just being certain that you two were still with me." Then he laughed. "Maybe the whores on the border will be glad to see us."

"When you got money, them bitches always are excited to see you. Why, they will piss in their panties to see hombres with *dinero*."

"So that they don't find out how much we have."

"Ah, *sí*, there are more bandits in Mexico than flies at the marketplace."

"We need to be very careful that no one knows about our money."

"Guerra and I know that, Señor. You don't have to doubt our loyalty for one second. We could have taken that money, fled for Mexico, and no one would have known who had it. We work for you, Señor."

Toby nodded. They could have done that. Just so they didn't get any new ideas about abandoning him and taking the loot. Sumbitch. He had that to worry about, as well as whoever was on his ass. If Earl Simpson was alive, he would be looking for Toby. And, Toby figured, the Texas law would be on his tail, especially if they checked back at the ranch and found that he'd pulled out.

In two days, they'd be well across the border in a village the boys knew well called Matador Negro. It was to be his headquarters until they could find a ranchero for him or someplace better. The boys felt certain the village would be defensible, and they knew the locals well enough. Valdez had agreed, and he was the most loyal of Toby's ranch help. In a few days, Valdez would join them with the rest of his things. Toby would sleep better when his man was with them. But they were all good boys. Mexico would be fun. He had the money and the team to ranch or do whatever he desired to do.

Mainly hump some sweet ass. It had been days since he'd had any. He never liked to be without pussy for long. It soured his disposition. However, they would celebrate when they got down there. He reached inside his pants and straightened his growing erection. Simply thinking about wild women had aroused him. Damn, he would be horny by the time they got to Matador Negro.

They stayed the night at a small ranch. The man, a gringo, only had a brush arbor for a house, and corrals were made of small, crooked mesquite poles strung between double posts. The man charged them twenty-five cents per horse for hay, since he said he had to have it hauled from forty miles away down in Mexico. With a scruffy white beard, he looked up in years, but still acted spry considering how old he must be. His cowboy hatband was black from sweat, and the caked-on dirt was piled around the crown. His spurs were Mexican rowels, his pants deerskin, and the shirt a pullover. He smoked cigarettes rolled in corn husks, and his thin lips were white from sun scars. But his deep blue eyes never missed a detail. He carried two large knives and an old cap-and-ball pistol called a Paterson model.

"I almost forgot how to talk English," the old man said between puffs on a cigarette.

"Is she Mexican or Indian?" Toby indicated the short young woman in the pleated skirt and thin low-cut blouse. Her small breasts could be seen when she bent over to stir the frijoles.

"Who knows?" The old man, who called himself Hodges, shrugged his thin shoulders. "You want some of her, you pay her. She came here starving. Her baby died the next day. She is hardworking and doesn't go hungry here. But at my age, I don't need a woman very often."

Toby nodded. He hoped he never lived to be so old that he didn't need one.

"Sofia," Hodges said, and she raised up to look at him. "After supper, he wants to buy some of your ass." His words to her were in Spanish, and she blushed.

"*Sí*, if he wants me."

She went back to her stirring and fussing.

"There, you have a deal," Hodges said to Toby.

Seated on his butt on the dirty blanket, Toby nodded. "I'll buy some of her. One of you boys go get us some whiskey. Hodges needs a good snort for looking out for me."

The old man nodded his head in approval. "I ain't had any whiskey in years."

Soon, they ate her corn tortillas and frijoles with hot sauce, and drank whiskey to wash it down. Afterwards, she took a rolled-up blanket under her arm and came over to get Toby as if it was business as usual. Then she led him a hundred yards off in the low greasewood and pear so that he no longer heard the voices of his men or Hodges as the sun set.

After cleaning the area of sticks, she unfurled the blankets on the sandy ground. "What do they call you?"

"Toby," he said, seated on his butt, pulling off his boot.

"My name is Sofia. I come from the mountains."

"You have a family in the mountains?"

"Who knows? I have not been there in a long time. Bandits may have killed them." She was busy untying the strings that held her skirt on her small waist. When that garment was shed, her dark legs looked shapely in the growing twilight. The blouse came off over her head, and her small triangular tits shook when it did.

"All I have left is that old man." On her knees in front of Toby, she took off his vest and then began undoing the buttons on his shirt. He fondled her breasts. It felt good to have flesh again in his palms to knead. Her nipples quickly responded to his attention. With his hand on her firm butt, he pulled her in close to feast on her nipples. This would be well worth what he would pay her.

With his gun holster laid aside, he stood, and she unbuckled his pants. Then she fought his pants down until the night wind swept his bare legs. Raising up, she took his half-full erection in her mouth and blew on him so hard, she sent chills up his spine. Filled with excitement, he wanted to dance on his toes as she worked his manhood over with the hunger of a starved lioness.

As she squeezed his scrotum and then jerkied him off to speed him up, he knew he was coming and clutched her head. His efforts succeeded, and he came hard in her mouth. She scrambled to get on her back, wiping the streams of white from the corners of her mouth on the tops of her hands. At last, she grabbed his kerchief and swiped it all away. Then, she rested on her back, and raised her knees in the air for him to enter her.

Like a raging bear, he plunged his hard-on inside her wet twat, and went to pounding her ass as a new wave of raw need swept through him, driving himself deeper and deeper inside her tight slit as she hunched to meet him. Bare calloused heels pounded his back, and she moaned openmouthed as they sped off into oblivion. At last, the skin in the head of his dick felt stretched to breaking and he came again, this time deep inside her, like an exploding artillery shell. They collapsed in a pile.

After a short reprieve, they did it again, and afterward they fell asleep in each other's arms, until the night's chill awoke them under the thin blankets and they fled under the stars their separate ways to their own bedrolls in camp. He shivered for an hour until his body warmth rose enough to let him stop shaking so he could sleep.

Before the sun crept over some sawtooth range in the distance, she was up making the fire and cooking for all of them. Through sleep-deprived eyes, he considered slipping up behind her and inserting his dick in her while she fussed over things all bent over. But he never followed through.

After breakfast, he paid her ten dollars, and thought her eyes would bug out at the sight of such wealth in her small brown hands. She jumped up, pulled him down, and kissed him.

When the sun's long shadows pointed westerly, they rode south for the border and the Rio Grande. Guerra said they'd cross it by noon, and Matador Negro was only a short ways south of the international boundary formed by the Rio Grande River.

Gnawing on jerky, they forded the hock-deep river and climbed the sandy bank on the south side. He paused to look back. Soon, he'd be like Old Man Hodges and not remember how to speak English. But if they were all like Hodges's slut, Mexico was for him. Oh, he'd been there before and screwed his share of brown-skinned butts—but from that moment on, he'd better figure that Mexico was his land and their women were what he'd have to choose from.

Matador Negro was a sleepy place of jacales along some ditches that watered small fields of emerging corn and beans. Children ran about screaming in loud voices about visitors coming. A few scrawny chickens rushed to scratch in the horse turds left by his ponies for bits of grain or seeds. Some tethered milk goats along the banks of the irrigation ditches bleated like they wanted to get loose, straining at their collars.

Women came to their doorways and used the sides of their hands to shade their eyes from the bright sun to see the newcomers. Some of them were old and wrinkled. Many others bore swollen bellies. The rest, he saw, were too young to screw. But there would be suitable ones among the population for his needs.

They stopped at a cantina. Polo stayed with the horses. Toby and Guerra went inside.

"Ah, *mi amigo,* Jesus," Guerra said to the bartender, who looked excited to see his old friend. "This is my *patrón.*"

"Welcome to Matador Negro, Señor." He extended his hand to shake Toby's. "Oh, it is so good to have you here. What will it be, mescal or pulque?"

Tony knew the mescal was liquor—hard liquor. The pulque was a local beer tasting like sour mash that he hated. "Mescal," he said.

"*Sí, señor.* The first drink is on me."

"Thanks." Toby looked around at the dusty room. A scraggly set of deer antlers was hung on the wall behind the bar, a poorly stuffed javelina beside it with his tusks showing. And a mountain sheep skull with three-quarter-curled horns. The chairs were mismatched, and the tables had been carved on by knife bearers with such nasty pictures as a bearded man screwing a sheep or goat. The room sat empty.

Guerra and Jesus talked about finding a place to stay and soon Guerra told Toby, "We can buy or lease a ranchero twenty miles from here at a place called La Ciénaga Verde."

"How much to lease it?"

"He says a hundred dollars a year."

"How much to buy it?"

"Two thousand pesos."

"We will rent it. Find a few women to go with us."

Guerra nodded.

The deal was made, and in an hour three women were ready to go. Earlier, Toby had looked them over one at a time. Slouched in the captain's chair, he'd selected the three out of many who wanted go along and work for him. Nice to have women almost fighting to be his prize.

When he saw Teodora, a short girl with a bright smile, he whispered in her ear, "Can you fuck?"

She shouted, "Yes and often."

He figured he tall, dark-haired woman in her thirties with the straight back would be in charge of them. Her name was Teresa. And the last one, who chewed on her finger and whose brown eyes danced with excitement, was named Nana.

Burros were rounded up for them to ride. Teresa rode hers sideways as if she had a sidesaddle and looked very ladylike, which brought a sly smile to his face for having chosen her.

He decided they could defend themselves more easily at this ranchero, so they headed out. It was located at a place where springs bubbled up in the desert and there was water. In Africa they called it an oasis. He was concerned about the condition of the ranchero, but since they had adequate food supplies and pussy, who really cared.

Well past midnight, they reached the hacienda. Under the stars and moon they rode through the gate in the high wall. In the shadowy square, he dismounted and tried the pump at the tank. Water soon poured out of the wooden spout and he drank some. It was both cool and sweet. No chalky aftertaste.

The women joined him and also tasted the water. Nana soaked her head under the spout, and soon tossed water over everyone. Then she wrung out her hair.

"Where will we sleep? What will we do?" Questions flew.

He pointed the others toward Guerra and caught Nana by the sleeve. "You and I have a bedroll to share."

"Sí."

When he got his own bedroll loose from behind his cantle, she quickly assumed possession of it and led the way across the hard-packed ground to an unlighted building facing the square. Inside the dark room, she went looking for a ladder. "They used to sleep on the roof, no?"

"I guess so."

"Then we can, too."

He took the bedroll, afraid that she might fall with it,

and shouldered it himself to follow her up the rungs. They soon were on the roof and he agreed her plan was excellent. In no time at all, they both were naked and in the bedroll, him on top enjoying her body.

Afterward, they slept curled in a ball until dawn.

17

Juliana walked down the store aisle trying on her new boots.

"How do they fit?" Margie asked from on her knees where she'd been assisting Juliana's fitting.

"They're a little tight, but I've been in moccasins for a year. It'll take me some time to get used to them."

"At least we had some different sizes in those. Most of our shoes are one-size-fits-all. You have to use newspapers to fill out the difference."

Squatted on his heels to the side, Slocum smiled at her words. Margie might be fun to be around. Her tongue sounded honest and sharp.

Juliana told her, "I'll take them. Thanks, Margie."

"Good." She rose with a slight twist and then straightened, flexing her shoulders when she stood up. "I could use a good back rub this morning."

"Where does the line for that form?" Slocum asked, rising to his feet.

"You find it. You call me over," Margie said, and went off to get her charge pad.

"He owes them over a thousand dollars here. I had Margie check. Heavens," Juliana said privately to him. "I will be years paying these bills off."

"Maybe you should see the banker, too?"

"I don't know if I have the nerve. Lord only knows what he borrowed from the bank. What was he doing with all that money?"

"Having a high old time on your estate."

"We better check on the bank then, too."

Margie had returned with her receipt pad and swung back her hair. "I am so glad that you're back. I'm so sorry that I fainted, but I couldn't believe that he did that to you. I have know him for years. He once worked for my father on his ranch."

"I'm learning all sorts of things he did to me and others."

"Others?"

"I understand he kept the Woolsey girl at the house."

"Yes, they were to be married when the courts declared you legally dead."

"Anyway, I am certain there were others, now that I know so much more."

Margie shook her head. "Sorry, I can't help you. I'm either here working or at the ranch working there."

"You need a good man."

Hands on her hips, she surveyed Slocum and Carlos. "Which one do I get?"

Slocum held up his hands. "Excuse me. I need to get her settled."

"I'm-I'm with him, too," Carlos said, scrambling to get up.

"See? I can't find a man anywhere."

They laughed.

The three crossed the street to Texas National Bank. Carlos waited outside for them. A Mr. Cruthers invited her and Slocum inside his office. He was a slight man behind square glasses with weak-looking brown eyes and a serious set to his face. He showed them to chairs to sit on in front of his desk.

"How much does he owe here?" the man said, repeating her question. "Two thousand dollars and the interest."

She looked shaken by the news. "What did he need that much money for?"

"Said to buy some prize brood mares."

"I'm shocked," she said. "My family kept their bills paid. I wonder what he was thinking about."

"We expect, Mrs. Toby, the Hendley brothers to deliver a thousand head of your three-year-old steers to Kansas for a five percent commission," Mr. Cruthers said. "Cattle at the Abilene, Kansas, railhead have been selling in a range from seven to twelve cents per pound. At that rate, you should have an income from the sale this summer of between fifty thousand and a hundred-twenty thousand dollars to repay these notes."

Her tanned complexion faded and she put her hands to her mouth. "That much money?"

Cruthers nodded sharply. "Any more questions?"

"No," she said in a small voice.

"Will you need more money to operate on before then?" Cruthers asked.

"I'm not certain, sir."

"If you do, come see us. As you can see, we feel your operation is very creditworthy, Mrs. Toby."

"Thank you, sir."

Outside in the sun, she still looked shocked.

"You going to be all right?" Slocum asked.

"I'll be fine. I never realized what this Kansas cattle business meant, nor how much money could be made. A year or so ago when all this started, and before I was kidnapped, cattle were bringing two-fifty a head if you could sell them."

"Things have changed fast."

"I would say so. Let's get out to the ranch and see what a mess he has left me."

"You want a saddle?" he asked. "I mean, I never thought about it."

"No, I should have one at the ranch. Besides, I've not ridden on one in over a year. Like these boots, they'll take some getting used to as well."

Slocum laughed as they joined Carlos.

"What did you learn?" the youth asked.

"They aren't about to foreclose on her place yet."

"Good."

"He's teasing you," she said. "I have a thousand head of cattle headed for Kansas. We need to pray they make it."

"I can do that."

"Now we're going to the ranch and see what she has left."

Slocum boosted her up with his hands clasped together as a stirrup.

"You ever wonder back there why Margie Pitch fainted over hearing he'd sold me to the Comanche?" She reined her horse around.

"Just thought she was shocked that anyone would do that. Why? Do you think anything is out of place?"

"I'm thinking there is more there than we know about." She booted her pony to go. "Guess we won't ever know, will we?"

Slocum looked back at the store. "Maybe there is a way to find out."

The ranch headquarters looked like it was dripping in blood with the sun setting in the west. They dismounted in front of the house. Maria ran out to greet them, screaming, "The señora is alive! She is really alive. Oh, my, what a wonderful thing."

Juliana dismounted and hugged her. "I guess he's gone?"

"Early today. He rode in and rode out."

"Is his woman gone, too?" Julianne asked looking around for her.

"Piper Jordan came for her a few hours ago.."

"He needs her. Is Valdez gone also?"

"Yes, and he and Señor Toby took many things with them."

Juliana swung around to look at Slocum. "Guess we start over here."

He had his hat off, scratching his head. "It looks all right. Didn't burn down the house anyway."

"But it is a mess, Señor," said Maria. "Those men were just tramping through it."

"I bet they were. Carlos, put up the horses and make sure that area is all right. I'll go inside with her and see what they did in there."

"I can handle it." He gathered up the reins, then headed for the barns and pens.

"Should I close my eyes?" Juliana asked Maria.

"Oh, I am so sorry how things have gone here," Maria said.

"You couldn't stop them."

Broken glass crunched under his soles when Slocum stepped inside the vestibule. He stopped the women. "Wait until I sweep a path inside."

"That is not your job—"

He came back with a broom and swept the glass shards aside. The place did look ransacked. The places where pictures once hung were now lighter squares on the walls.

"Why did he take the portrait of me?" Juliana frowned at a vacant wall.

"They were like wolves in a lamb pen. Who knows why they took much of it?" Maria said, shaking her head.

"There is nothing we can do about that," Slocum said. "Are there still people working here?"

"Some," Maria said.

"Then ring a bell and get them up here. We are cleaning this house first. Then we will straighten out the livestock."

"Who rode up just now?" Juliana asked.

"I'll go see," Slocum said.

He walked to the open front door and saw a big man whose gut hung over the Mexican saddle horn. "Can I help you?"

"Yeah, where's Toby? He owes me six brood mares."

"How do you figure that?"

"Who in the hell are you? I want to talk to Toby."

"He's not here."

"Where did he go?"

"The sheriff would like to know that, too."

"Mister, he owes me—"

"You got a contract or receipt?"

"You know who I am?"

"No, who the hell are you?"

"Chester Knowles."

"I imagine with that name and ten cents, I could buy a cup of coffee in town. My name's Slocum. Now tell me why he owes you six brood mares."

Knowles made a scowling face. "I delivered six kegs of whiskey to a fella named Kelso Jennings for him a while back. Toby said to drop by and he'd pay me in brood mares."

"Why in the hell did he owe the one-eyed bastard whiskey anyway?"

"How in the hell am I supposed to know? He owes me six brood mares. You going to give them to me or we going to guns?"

"Keep your hand away from that gun's grips. Toby's on the run and he ain't here to pay you. Mrs. Toby is here and she ain't buying the whiskey story. I can tell you right now."

"Shit-fire, he said he'd pay me in them brood mares for that whiskey."

"You're a few days late. He came back from wherever and must have heard the sheriff wanted him and lit a shuck."

"You mean I'm out all that money?"

"Looks like it to me unless you can find him."

"What good would that do?"

"Damned if I would know," Slocum said, satisfied the man had indeed taken whiskey to Kelso and not gotten paid. The way Toby did business was to charge it. But Toby wasn't giving any whiskey to Kelso for his Indian whiskey business. Something else was going on. That worthless no-account whiskey trader—where did he fit in on this deal?

18

Toby sat drinking mescal on the porch of the house, knowing Valdez kept guards posted around the clock. No telling if some band of bandits had heard that a rich gringo was sitting on his ass down there. Why, they'd be there quicker than a lamb could switch his tail. He'd always have that worry about bandits as long as he stayed in this backward country. Maybe he could go to New Mexico or Arizona and hide there. Sumbitch. Richest man in the world and all he could do was worry—worry about *bandidos* learning about his wealth—worry about them coming and torturing him to find out where he hid the money.

He rose up, listening to those noisy birds. This place was a damn bird heaven. They chirped, sang, or made noises all day long. And here he sat, afraid to move or do anything. Maybe one of the women would distract him from feeling so low. Whenever anything was wrong with him, a woman in bed could usually clear it up or distract him enough that he forgot it.

"Ah, where is Teodora?" he said to the straight-backed Teresa in the kitchen.

"In her room. It is her time of the month," the woman said, not looking up.

Sumbitch. That was his luck. "Where is Nana?"

"She's in bed with a bad cold."

"What're *you* doing?" He'd never had any experience with the woman, but she wasn't ugly. In fact, she had a slender-looking body and might be just what he needed.

"Planning the evening meal."

"Hell with the evening meal." He swept her up in his arms and her eyes flew open in shock.

"What are you doing with me?"

"We are going to go and make love."

"But-but—you can do that with those girls. Put me down this minute."

He smiled hard at her. "They are not well, so you are the one."

With his boot, he kicked the bedroom door shut, crossed the room, and dumped her on the bed. "Get your clothes off or I'll shred them."

"I will, I will," she said, undoing the vest buttons while he pulled off his boots and watched her closely. She slithered the skirt down, then hurried to remove the black blouse. The chemise she pulled off over her head and then, naked, she reared up right in front of him. Her breasts sagged, capped with pointed black nipples. The creases ran across her flat belly. Her twat was behind a tuft of black hair.

He stepped in close and kissed her, running his hand between her legs to finger her. She widened her stance. She was dry, so he licked his fingers to probe her. In minutes, her breathing quickened and he bent over, feeding on her left breast. His finger found her clit, and she was hunching against his finger as her erection began to grow.

Then her arms went around his neck and her kissing grew wilder. He pushed her down on the edge of the bed, spread her legs, and drove his poker inside her. She let out a small scream as he pumped the fire out of her ass. Her thin legs soon were around him and she was meeting his every thrust—then he heard the pop of guns. He rose above her.

"What in the hell is going on?"

"Oh, oh," she moaned, out of breath, the side of her hand

to her forehead and she sprawled on her back. "You better go see. It could be bandits."

He pulled on his pants. Those low-life bastards coming in and breaking up his pleasure—he'd show them. With the black powder cap-and-ball Colt in his fist, he started down the tile-floored hall, listening to more shots and horses galloping around outside.

He went to the three open windows in the dining room, and saw one rider dressed as a vaquero go by with a smoking gun. The next one who came by he shot off his horse. Then he slipped through the open window, and ran to get the pistol of the one he'd just shot, hoping it was loaded. Stickers jabbed his tender feet. He heard a raider scream and charge his horse right at him before he reached the downed one.

The blast of a shotgun tore the outlaw off his black horse with its silver-mounted saddle. Toby looked at the window. There, wearing only the white chemise, Teresa stood with the still-smoking shotgun to her shoulder. He made a bow at her, then ran to get both men's handguns. Damn her hide, she did well.

He heard two more mounted raiders coming around the corner of the house. He took aim and shot the first one in the chest. The bullet caused the man to spread his arms out and then to cartwheel off the back of his horse.

His next shot was a misfire and when the hammer clicked, the sound made him instantly sick to his stomach. The gun-bearing bandit on horseback bore right down on him. Then the shotgun again roared from the house. The second rider screamed and fell off his mount. His horse, obviously hit, too, half reared, and then fell on top of its own rider on the ground.

Toby shouted, "Stay down," at Teresa.

He went to the front, and found two more dead or dying outlaws on the ground. There was no more shooting or shouting.

Polo joined him, looking concerned. "I looked all over for you."

"I know. I was busy." He chuckled, and Polo nodded to indicate that he knew where he had been.

"Are they all dead?" his man asked.

"Be sure no one lives to talk of this day. It would only bring more trouble here."

"*Sí, señor.*"

"Where is Valdez?"

'I think he was taking a siesta, Señor."

"Good. Be sure they are all dead, and the horses that are hurt bad, do the same. Have my new silver saddle put safely away."

"Oh, you got him, too, huh? What else?"

"Break out a few bottles of mescal and celebrate. We won this war."

He went in the kitchen, bent over, scooped Teresa up by the calves of her legs so she was well over his head, and headed for the bedroom with his prize.

"But I must fix food—"

"Not yet." At the bedroom door, he let her slip down in his arms to kiss her. Then, inside the room, he set her on the edge of the bed and shed his pants. One of his newly acquired guns clunked on the floor before he could catch it. His pants off, he shoved her down on her back, threw the gown up, spread her legs, and with his dick in his fist, drove it home inside of her.

In seconds, they were back to their wildfire fury and he felt the eruption coming. The explosion burned a hot track of fire from his scrotum, and then flew out the head of his dick like a grenade.

She cried out and half fainted on her back. He crawled off her and went belly-down on the bed.

Completely spent, he reached for her.

She pulled away. "I must go fix them some food—the men. They all worked hard—"

"Yes, they did. Come sleep with me tonight when you go to bed."

"If you wish me to."

"I wish you to."

"I will."

Good. He closed his eyes and fell sound asleep for the first time in days.

19

Must have been getting near the full moon. Slocum could not sleep that evening, and walked the hall floors, which were washed in bright moonlight. Barefooted, he strode the tile looking for answers to where Earl Simpson had gone. If Toby had his money, maybe Earl had gone looking for him. But there had been no sign of Simpson, as far as Slocum knew, since they'd been at Fort Concho.

He and Juliana rode away from up there, and from what he could find out, her husband Toby came through, then Simpson, and last but not least, the Pinkerton men rode by there. Toby came home, loaded up, and vamoosed. Pinkertons showed up in Decore looking for Simpson. So somewhere, Simpson threw a kink in his rope and managed to avoid all of them.

There had to be an answer. In the morning, he'd ride into Decore and see if he could learn anything. Ready to try and sleep, he went back to the feather bed and Juliana's soft sleeping form. In minutes, he fell into a restless sleep. Up before dawn, he was in the kitchen with Maria, who poured him coffee and fed him.

"You tell her I needed to go do some checking. She still has plenty of work to do on her books. Carlos will be certain that nothing happens to her. I'll be back late tonight or tomorrow and not to worry."

"Oh, she will worry, it is a woman's way."

He rode a ranch horse to Decore, his Spencer under the right fender in the scabbard and the .44 on his hip. He found that Margie had the store open and was sweeping the aisles.

"You the only one here?" he asked, looking around to be certain they were alone.

"Yes. How is Juliana?"

"Fine. Doing fine. How are you?"

"All right—but—I am being blackmailed by a man," she said in a soft whisper. "A whiskey trader named Kelso. You know him?" She rose on her toes to look for anyone coming.

"How can he do that?"

She looked wary about answering, but at last she said, "I was having an affair with Job Toby. He and I had this thing from way before he ever married Juliana. I'm sorry and embarrassed that I let it go on. But Toby threatened to expose me unless I did what he demanded. Kelso must have learned about it and now he wants in on the deal."

"What's Kelso demanding?"

"Some money, but the rest you can imagine." She looked embarrassed.

"When will he come around again?"

"When I go home at noon to take a short break, he'll show up today because that's been my schedule."

"He's coming today?"

"I think so. Oh, Slocum, I hate to bother you, but I have no one else to turn to. Dad will be coming to work any minute. Kelso will ride in the back gate, put his mule in the barn, and slip in the house by the back door."

"Draw me a map to the house." He motioned to the butcher paper and she scribbled one on a piece of it.

"Dad never comes home at noon," she said. Then she slipped him the detailed map.

"Why Miss Pitch, I sure do thank you for that information on those detectives," Slocum said, loud enough that she understood that her father had just come in the back door.

"Father, you remember Slocum, with the Pinkerton Detective Agency? We haven't seen those other two in town again, have we, Father?" she called out to him.

"You need them Slocum?" he asked, putting on his fresh apron for the day.

"Oh, I wanted to share some ideas with them about Job Toby. But it was nothing. I better get along."

"Juliana still doing well?"

"Yes, sir, she's getting herself and her ranch back in shape."

"A fine girl. It's such a shame she'll bear that cross for the rest of her life."

"What cross is that?" Slocum asked, struck with a tinge of anger.

"You know what I mean."

"Only if people crucify her for what she didn't do. She didn't choose those bucks."

"It will be a stigma nonetheless."

He left the store halfway pissed at Pitch's attitude and sorry he hadn't finished the conversation with his daughter. But obviously, he needed to clear Kelso out of her life—regardless.

The map was easy to understand. Kelso would come in the back gate sometime and ride up to the back of the barn, stable his mule inside, and then go inside the house to wait for her. The gate Kelso entered by was a half mile north off the road that joined Beulah Street. On the east side of the ranch was Horn Road, which ran alongside Hurst Creek. Slocum could go up there and cross the creek to an obvious wire gate. Then come back down to the house through the willows that were tall enough to conceal him and his pony.

He used her directions after he left the store. He knew he probably had hours before Kelso would come, if he did show up. She'd sounded convinced that the whiskey trader would be there that day to harass her.

Like a Comanche buck, he came up through the willows leading his pony. He looked over the pens and decided to put his horse in the back one. Make him look like he was a horse Pitch had taken in trade. Slocum unsaddled, stowed his rig out of sight, and put the gelding in the far pen with water and hay. After he rolled in the dirt, the gelding would look like he belonged there.

Slocum went on to the house. If Kelso came in the back door, he'd be sitting on a kitchen chair in the shadows, ready for his arrival. He was all set up with his .44 in his lap when he finally heard the mule bray and then Kelso smother the sound.

He hoped his horse wouldn't draw enough attention for Kelso to go over and check on it. The windup clock in the living room chimed eleven o'clock. Soon, he heard the gritty scratch of rawhide boot soles on the back steps. His plan was working. The knob turned and the back door eased inward with a soft protest of the hinges.

"Don't move a muscle," Slocum ordered.

20

"I'll kill every one of you bastards!' Every one of you—"

"Wake up. Wake up. You've been having nightmares," Teresa said, shaking Toby by the shoulders.

Trembling all over, he sat up and tried to clear his brain. His fuzzy vision only added to his plight. What was wrong? Where was he? Nighttime. In bed with Teresa. He reached over, hugged her, and closed his sore eyes.

Hoping the tremors would soon leave, he wrapped his arms tighter around her. "I thought I was . . ."

She wiped his face with her hand and then straightened his hair. "It will pass. It will pass."

Still shaking like a dog trying to pass a peach seed, he let go of her, dropped his head, and slowly shook it. "Guess I was redoing the war we had here yesterday."

"You must have been," she said, running her palm down the side of his face and making him look at her. "You need to relax more. You are worrying too much. Now relax your feet."

"What'll this do?"

"It will give you relief. Think about relaxing your feet."

"I am."

"Think harder. I feel your feet twisting under the covers."

"I'm trying."

Gradually, she worked up his body section by section, and even his heart rate slowed to a leisurely pace. Then she rolled him on his belly, and her hands began to knead the tension and tightness out of his shoulder muscles. No one had ever massaged him before, not like this woman, and he fell deeper and deeper into an abyss. Soon, he felt like a cooked noodle as she worked lower and lower down his body. His hips . . . He fell into a deep slumber.

Past sunup, he awoke—and reached out to find her. She was gone. Damn. He sat up on the edge of the bed and wiped his face with his dry palms. For the first time in ages, he felt like his old self again—the woman was good. Better than any doctor he'd ever visited. Maybe she was a witch— a *bruja*.

Who cared? His body didn't ache where he once broke his leg or his arm busting broncs. His right elbow felt all right when he flexed it. He quickly dressed and went to locate her.

He found her in the kitchen cooking for everyone. She was bent over busy baking biscuits in the stove oven. He poured his own coffee.

"Morning."

"Morning," she said without looking up.

"I feel so much better."

"Today, I will have the men help me build a sweat lodge. There is still poison in your pores we must draw out."

"Fine. Fine," he said, blowing on his coffee. "Where did you learn all this?"

"From a medicine man."

"He was a good teacher." He tried to sip some of the brew. Still too hot.

Valdez soon joined him. "We have the bandits all buried and the horses have been ridden over the ground until there is no sign left of their graves."

"Did the men recognize any of them?"

"No. Simply bandits."

"You did well. We were ready for them," Toby said.

She brought Valdez his coffee.

"Gracias. How did you sleep, Teresa?" Valdez asked her.

"Very well, very well."

Valdez turned back to Toby. "How long should we stay here?"

"A few more days. She wants me to take a sweat bath." He indicated Teresa. "After that, we can move on. How many days will the sweat baths take?"

"Three days?" She turned and looked at them.

"Fine, we can stay here that long," Toby said, anxious to recover from all that was troubling him.

"Fine. We will sleep with our eyes open," Valdez said.

Toby nodded his thanks to his *segundo* for understanding—this was important to him.

So he sat in the sweat lodge and they brought extremely hot rocks to dump in his water vessels. There was the smell of cedar oil in the air inside the confines of the canvas-covered hut. Each day, he emerged after several hours and she massaged his muscles.

Things looked clearer when he came out of his lodge. His mind grew sharper about things. The bad decisions he made in the past grew smaller in his conscience. Somewhere he would build a great ranch—Mexico was just a hotbed of bandits. Perhaps in northern New Mexico, he could find a place.

Ah, her hands were drawing the tension out of the muscles again.

In a week, they loaded up and moved out. Valdez and his men had the pack train better organized. Many of the less valuable items were left behind, like the large portrait of his wife. Why in the hell did he ever take it along? There was no good reason for it to burden an animal any longer.

Toby led the train as they moved westward toward El Paso. He knew the King's Highway north to Santa Fe was long and dry, but probably the best route for his train to take. The Rio Grande River would provide water.

His money was packed on the bay gelding.

21

"You move one inch and you're dead meat, Kelso Jennings."
Slocum pointed the cocked .44 at his back.

"That you, Slocum? You taking another woman away from me?"

Slocum, gun ready, slipped behind the man, who had his hands in the air, jerked out the man's .45 Navy Colt, stuck it in his own waistband, and then took three large knives off the man, before he shoved him out into the sunlight that had been filtering into the kitchen.

"What's the deal? What's the deal?" Kelso kept asking.

"Blackmail she called it."

"I never—I was just filling in for Toby. Him being gone, I figured she needed some company."

"You're blackmailing her."

"Naw, I just wanted to rut a little with her."

"Tell me about Toby."

"I ain't seen my old buddy in weeks. What's he up to?"

"I imagine he's having a high old time somewhere down there below the border."

"That sumbitch got all the money that Simpson and them boys took off that cattleman up in Kansas, didn't he?"

"Toby never shared any of it with you?"

"Hell, no. I looked for him, but he was already gone and you had the ranch back."

"You seen Simpson?"

"No. I ain't looked for him either. He's lucky. Them Messicans of Toby's used a wooden vise on them other two's nuts to find out what they wanted to know. Guess that's how they got the money." Kelso shook his head. "That's as mean as anything I ever heard about."

"Tell me about a man named Chester and a horse deal Toby made with him."

"I needed some more whiskey to go out and trade some more. You costed me several barrels. I said I'd help Toby find his damn wife that you had if he'd buy me six kegs of lightning. Chester showed up with it. Guess Toby paid him in horses for it."

"Interesting. I'm taking you to the jail in Mason and turning you over to the federal judge on charges of selling firewater to Indians. The deputy U.S. marshal can haul your ass down to San Antonio for your trial. But you say one word about Margie Pitch's reputation and you're dead meat. I can have you killed in prison as well as outside. You savvy?"

"I savvy good. My mouth is shut. I only wanted a little pussy."

"Well, you chose the wrong one to mess with."

"You know, I ought to hate you. First, you take that stupid, silent bitch away from me. He'd've paid me a lot for her. And now you're sending me up over *this* gal. But I don't hate you. You're a smooth bastard and you've outfoxed me twice."

"Where did Simpson go?"

Kelso turned up his hands. "I ain't seen him. But you can bet your sweet ass he's out there somewhere figuring out how to get all of his money back and not get his balls mashed and throat slashed like them boys of his did."

Slocum heard a rig pulling up outside. He went to the window and drew the lace curtain aside. It was Margie by herself, like she'd said. From his place, he watched her get down, hitch the buggy horse to the post, and come carrying her skirt out of the dust on her way to the porch.

When the front door opened, Slocum said, "Come in here, Margie. We're in the kitchen."

She came in to the room fluffing her hair up. Her brown eyes narrowed and her mouth drew in a tight line. "Oh, you've already got that rotten blackmailer."

"All I wanted was a little loving," said Kelso.

With an angry scowl, she glared at him. "And some money."

Kelso shrugged. "Well, I was broke."

Slocum interrupted. "I promised him if he even so much as mentioned your name, I'd personally have him killed in or outside of prison. And I can do that—he knows me well."

Her teeth obviously gritted, she looked hard at the whiskey trader. Hard enough that if her looks were sending bullets, he would have been dead right there. "You better not ever come into my life again. I'd like to shoot you right here, you've made me so mad."

"You've got my word, lady. I won't be back. Ever."

"It better be good. I'm telling you."

"Be careful and don't step on his knives," Slocum said. "They're on the floor. Sorry, I had no place else to put them."

She swept up a bowie knife and put it on the dry sink. "This one would cut it all off flush with his belly."

Kelso grabbed for his crotch.

They ate a quiet lunch of rye bread and ham. When it was over, Slocum headed his prisoner for the back door.

Kelso stopped and looked back. "Even after all this trouble you've caused me, I think you'd've been a good piece of ass."

With his stiff arm, Slocum shoved him out the door onto the porch. "Shut up."

"Slocum," she called after him. "Thank you is all I can say."

"That's enough."

In the barn, Kelso made a fast move for him, but not quick enough. It ended with a pistol muzzle jammed into the trader's belly, and Slocum asked, "And now you want to die?"

"No. No."

"Good 'cause you just came within an inch of getting there. Don't try me again. You won't survive the outcome." They went and got Slocum's horse and saddled him, then led him out.

Kelso dropped his shoulders in defeat and got his mule out of the stall. They rode off for Mason.

The sheriff's deputy took down the information and locked Kelso up in a cell.

"He'll be here until the deputy U.S. marshal comes by for him," said the deputy sheriff. "Who gets the federal reward on him?"

"Mrs. Juliana Toby."

"I'll see that she gets it, or the sheriff will."

Slocum thanked the man and left the jail. Stars were already out. It would be late when he got back to the ranch, but that didn't matter. He had Kelso behind bars, and that was one problem out of his way. Why did he think that Earl Simpson was still around there? No proof or word of anyone sighting him. But these people didn't know him except from a vague description of a man on a poster.

Simpson was still in the country? Call it gut feeling, but those notions usually turned out to be right.

The next morning at breakfast with Juliana, he went over his day with Margie and his arrest of Kelso.

"I imagine she was pleased to be rid of that stinking whiskey trader." Juliana shook her head as if the smell of him was still in her nose.

"I wanted you to know that Margie apologized to you about her affair with Toby. It was not a new one and went way back. He blackmailed her, too, she said."

"I don't doubt anything underhanded that Job Toby did behind my back. Obviously, I was the biggest blind fool in this country. Since coming back, I have even learned he had a child with a woman who worked here in the house. Probably did it in my own bed for all I know."

"I'm sorry."

"No need for you to be sorry. I never knew it was going on either before I learned all about the rest of the rotten things that he did. It was all concealed from me. I wonder who else he had affairs with."

He shook his head, reading the upset in her blue eyes. She rose up and came over to sit in his lap and wept on his shoulder.

"I'll never run this ranch. What can I do?"

"We can hire you a good foreman. There's top men would give their right arm to run an operation like yours. Sure, it would take him time to build a crew and gather cattle, brand the ones that got away."

"I have no money."

"You have credit with Mr. Cruthers that will be covered by the cattle sale this summer. We'll round up all of his debts, get them paid, and then when the money comes in, you will be out of debt and have plenty of operating money."

"What about Knowles?" she asked, wiping her tears away with a cloth from her pocket.

"Your husband made that debt, according to Kelso, to repay him for the whiskey he lost when I won you away from him. Let's see what he'd take in cash instead of the horses."

She agreed. "I'll get dressed and we can look all these people up. The debt I hate to pay the most is to the dress shop for that other woman's clothing."

"It was his debt."

"I know. I know. That no-good son of a bitch anyway."

"Get it out of your system. He's gone. He won't be back. Flush him out."

"I will. I'll do that very thing. You know, I gave him all of this. He was busting horses for two dollars a head." She shook her head. "And this is how he repaid me, having affairs, spending my money—the ranch's money, like it was water. Do you think he had anything to do with my father's death?"

"You said he was killed in a wagon wreck?"

"Yes, he was thrown from the seat and had a bad blow to his head. We thought he struck a rock. But I never checked. Oh, if he murdered him, I'd kill him with my bare hands."

"It would be hard to prove this late."

She agreed. "Will you ride along with me? We'll make a list of all the debts he owes people and see if we can pay them off. Oh, and you can start looking for a ranch foreman. You wouldn't take that post, would you?"

"I'd love to but—I have some problems in my past. They might come haunt me if I stayed too long here."

"Oh. I'm going to cry when you leave me."

"Don't. Time comes I'll have to leave, it will be as simple as that."

"But-but what will I do?"

"Find someone else. You're young and attractive. You could have your pick of men."

"Even with the Comanche curse on me?"

"A man who comes along and loves you won't ever mention it."

"I wish I thought that was true."

"It will be if you can make it so."

"Let's go find out about those debts."

They went by Knowles's place first. A woman hardly out of her teens came to the doorway in a dress unbuttoned down the front that she held closed at her navel with one hand.

"He ain't 'chere."

"Tell him," Slocum said, "that we were by and Mrs. Toby wants to settle with him."

"I'll sure tell him that for sure." She let the hand go that held the dress shut and smiled big at him. "Come back again."

"Who is she?" he asked when they were halfway down the lane to the road.

"I guess his new wife. His other one died in childbirth. You see enough?"

"Too much." Slocum chuckled and they rode on.

The man at the mill told them that Job Toby's debt on the

books was 460 dollars, and he had not settled the ranch's bill in over a year.

"We'll handle that," she said, and made a note.

"Ma'am, I'd sure appreciate you doing that. I'm a small businessman and carrying a bill like this sure has hurt me."

"Consider it paid, sir."

By the end of the day, she found her husband owed almost six thousand dollars, including his horse loan, if they allowed Knowles thirty dollars a barrel for the whiskey. That was all that Slocum wanted to pay the man.

"Who else do you think he might owe?" she asked.

"We have the main people. You show Cruthers the list and we'll see what he says."

"What if he turns us down?"

"There's more bankers in Texas."

"You're serious, aren't you?"

"Yes, I am."

She made a half smile and they went in the front door of the bank. Thirty minutes later, she had the money to pay off her creditors. Still acting a little shocked, she carried the money in her purse over to Pitch's, where she cleared away that bill. Then they rode down to the mill and paid the dust-floured miller the amount she owed him.

He took off his cloth cap and bowed to her. "I sure am beholden. You need anything, you let me know any time, ma'am."

After leaving the mill, she said, "Tomorrow we can go to Mason and I'll clear up those debts."

Slocum agreed.

"It's a shame you don't have your bedroll along."

"Shame? Why's that?"

"We'd just camp somewhere out here tonight and forget the ranch."

"Next time, I'll sure bring it along."

She looked a little embarrassed as they rode on. "I'm sorry. I guess I wanted to escape."

"Nothing wrong with wanting to escape every once in

a while." He closed his eyes. "Nothing wrong at all with that."

They were back at the ranch in late afternoon. Carlos met them at the house.

"How did it go today?" Slocum asked.

"Fine. I sent three boys out to check the north range, to look over the cattle, and get a count on how many calves on the ground that we have to brand. They'll make top hands in a few years. Besides, these boys have done a lot of the ranch work around here the past year. Those pistoleros lounged around all day."

"Sounds like you have things going all right."

She agreed with a nod and swung down off her horse.

"One more thing," said the boy. "Two tough white men came by and asked if she was home. Wouldn't tell me their names and got kind of mouthy."

"Did Maria or any of the others know them?"

"No. But they were hard cases. I couldn't figure what they wanted with her."

"Good question. Keep your hand gun handy. We're going into Mason tomorrow and do some business. Maybe we should arm a few of the vaqueros to back you in case they come back."

"I can do that. We need guards at night yet?"

"I hope not."

"These boys are serious about their jobs. They want to be vaqueros. All I need to say is we should guard some at night and they'd jump in to help to be sure that we were all safe."

"Arm the guards with Spencers from the house. Be sure they all know how to use them. While there aren't a lot of guns left that Toby didn't take, there are a handful. They can pass on their rifles to the men who relieve them on guard duty."

"I'll do it."

Slocum and Juliana went to the house. Carlos hurried to set up his guards.

"Who were those men asking about me?"

"Search me. But we need to be more careful. Ride some back roads where they don't expect to find you."

She agreed, and they went in the kitchen to see Maria.

"How was your day, Maria?" Juliana asked.

"There were two tough hombres here today who asked about you. They got pushy with Carlos when he stood up to them."

"Who were they?" asked Slocum.

"I don't know, but why would they come asking for her?"

"It don't make much sense. They must have known her husband was gone or they'd've asked for *him*."

"It worried me all day. I don't want her hurt anymore." Maria looked upset.

"I think we have things in hand now. I'll have a few armed men stay around to back Carlos when we are gone."

Who were they? Why ask for her? That was strange. He'd poke around some and find some answers. Someone knew who they were, and he would have that information in a day or so. He entered the bedroom and tossed his felt hat on a chair.

"You feeling better?" he asked as Juliana stood before the tall mirror and brushed her shoulder-length hair.

"Yes, some. Now I must hope and pray the cattle all arrive safely in Kansas, huh?" She twisted to look back at him. "Am I being too vain looking at myself in this tall mirror he bought for her?"

"You looked at your image for months and never spoke. Now you can watch yourself and speak as well."

She threw her head back and laughed. "Maybe that is why I like the mirror so much."

He came up behind her and hugged her around the neck. "Next time, I'll take a bedroll."

"Hey, there is nothing that we can't do in that bed to-night." She pulled harder on her brush. "Why did he need so many other women?"

"To some men, women are conquests. The more you have, the bigger you are."

She nodded sharply. "They fed his ego, right?"

"They must have. Why?"

"I thought I had failed him as a wife for months out there while I was being poked by young bucks. I thought that was the reason why he sent me off. I was such a poor excuse for a wife. But it wasn't that at all. He had my ranch, and he got rid of me to get another ranch. It wasn't our sex in bed. It wasn't my fault at all, was it?"

"I think you hit the nail on the head, girl."

She tossed the brush aside and hugged him. "Gawdamn him anyway."

And she began to weep on Slocum's shirt.

If she ever cried hard enough, she might get over it.

22

Toby and his crew spent little time in El Paso, and rode on to Mesilla. Toby stayed in the Los Cruces Hotel on the south side of the square and market in the middle of town. There were several loud Americans in the bars.

"Now if they'd turn the Union army on these red pissant Apaches, this country would be cleared in six months. Bunch of blanket-assed fuckers anyway. The army could show them like they did Lee, only ten times faster."

Toby heard them all the while he was sipping whiskey and fondling some young whore in a booth. He'd soon shove her under the table, slouch down, undo his pants, and let her suck on him. Those braggarts had no idea about the Western Indian—they were the most cold-blooded killers ever invented. He'd seen a driver tied on a coach wheel upside down and his brains had been boiled out of his skull over a mesquite fire. Toby imagined that they sat there on their haunches and watched him die with expressionless faces until he stopped screaming.

He gave Teresa some money to shop with. She bought a new white blouse, a black vest, a long divided black riding skirt, and a straw sombrero against the sun. She looked very stylish in her new outfit, and he could not complain about her wild ways in bed. But he knew little about her past.

Had she ever been married? He thought so. She was no virgin when he first mounted her. But she was no common whore. If she ever had been one—it had been high-class. She never spoke of children or a home. But he found he really liked a woman who was intelligent enough to talk with when it was over.

His new plans included going to Silver City next. The road from Mesilla to Lordsburg was dangerous, but he had many good shooters. Maybe he could find a business up there to invest in. What did he know about business? Teresa might know about business. He'd ask her in bed that night.

Later, on top of her, he spoke in her ear. "You know about business?"

"Sure. What kind?"

"The kind that makes lots of money."

She laughed. "You need to have a saloon and whorehouse in a rich goldfield town to do that."

"Silver City rich enough?"

"I think so. I don't know, but it might be. I've never been there."

He laughed and poked her harder. "We're going there next."

He had six good men, well armed, plus Valdez and himself. They were down to Teresa and Nana to do the cooking and camp care. Teodora and one of his men named Claudio had ridden off together one night for El Paso. He armed his men with Spencer repeating rifles and lots of ammo and tubes. They were much longer-lasting than the brass works in the Henry repeater, which wore out quickly and then jammed. Besides the .45 Navy Colt each man wore on his waist, each man had two more in saddle holsters on each side of his saddle horn. Even when armed to the teeth, crossing the lower end of the New Mexico Territory with a small band of men was like waving a flag at all the Apaches in the country.

They left in the predawn. With their horses all shod and

grained, they made a lightning force as they trotted westward when they left the Mesilla Valley. The five-day trip proved uneventful, and they soon arrived in Silver City. The place was alive with miners, gamblers, pickpockets, con men, and busy whores. Gold dust was the choice currency, and the faro wheels spun twenty-four hours a day in the gambling halls.

Valdez found them a large casa on the small stream that ran through the village. The man wouldn't sell it, but offered to rent it for thirty dollars a month. There was a place for their horses, sheds, and a corral. The house had many rooms inside, and there was a wall around the place that made it look like a fort. The property had once belonged to a rich Spaniard—no word on why he had moved or abandoned it.

Set up in the casa, Toby and Teresa, with Polo as a bodyguard or taking Guerra along, began to look at businesses to invest in. A man named Kelly wanted to sell his saloon, but all his *putas* worked in tents out behind on a stony hillside. Teresa thought it would be too much trouble to keep things under control and collect the money due them.

A large mercantile wanted to sell. The place was swamped with customers from sunup to late at night, but when Teresa looked at their books, she told Toby they were carrying too many mining companies that were not paying on a regular basis. Besides, they wanted Toby to pay a hundred percent for all the credit being carried on those books.

Toby felt he was learning a lot about business. Teresa could spot things like, in the crude bar under the palm fronds, the bartenders pocketed too much of the money that patrons paid them for beer.

He never knew there were so many ways to screw an owner before—he learned those tricks listening to her. They looked at a large, boarded-up building on the way into town. When they peered through the cracks in between the boards and the dust-coated glass, it looked to be a usable enough structure. They found the owner and met with him. A Yankee named Paul Coats who acted aloof, smoked cigarettes in holders, and wore a monocle. His fluffy silk scarf was wrapped around his neck and he was dressed in a starched white suit.

"Oh, you are talking about the Clyde building," he said. "Oh, I must talk to my financial advisor, Señor Sanchez, before I sell anything. He's gone to Santa Fe this week on business. So—" He reset his eyepiece and looked them over again. "There is nothing I can do until he returns."

Coats rose with his gold-capped cane and strolled out, leaving them with the bill for lunch and the drinks.

"Who does that bastard think he is?" Toby demanded.

Teresa caught his arm and restrained him. "He's a spoiled remittance man."

"What's that mean?"

"They are the younger sons in a family and the first son gets the estate over there in Europe. The first sons support the younger sons, but the younger sons have to live in exile."

"I'll be damned. What now, Teresa?"

"We learn where Coats banks. If he owns the building, he may not have enough money to make it a business. A bank might be ready to foreclose on it, too."

"Where do you find that out?" Toby asked.

"The courthouse has a record of all liens."

"Good. I never thought about that."

They learned that Coats owed two thousand dollars on the building to the Miner's Bank. Teresa smiled when they came out in the sunshine. "It is hardly worth more than the two thousand. Offer the bank fifteen hundred dollars and see what they will do."

"You think they'd take that much less?"

She nodded like it would be nothing for them to accept the bid.

A short man in the bank named Engles took them into his private office. He listened to Toby's story about the building and what he'd pay for it. Then Engles leaned back in his chair, folded his hands on his vest, and smiled. "I would accept eighteen hundred dollars for it."

Toby looked at Teresa. She nodded, and he agreed to give that much.

"Will it be a bank transfer?" Engles asked.

"No, I sold my ranch in Texas. We'll have the money— cash."

"My, my. I didn't know there was that much money left in Texas."

"There was," Toby said, and after setting the date for closure, they left the bank.

Outside in the sunshine, he hugged her shoulder. "Damn, where did you learn about all this business?"

"My late husband."

"He must have been real smart."

"He was."

They went back to the casa for supper. Toby wondered who he had been—her husband.

23

A week later, a man drove up to the 345 Ranch in a buggy. He wore a snap-brim hat and was dressed in a tailored business suit. Slocum was at the barn shoeing a horse. He had seen the man coming, then washed his hands in the horse tank, and was drying them on a sack while headed downhill to see who he was and what he wanted.

"I am looking for a man named Slocum," the man said.

"I'm Slocum," he said, being joined by the rifle-carrying Carlos, who looked the man over.

"Expecting trouble here?" The man looked around.

"We've had some."

"Well." He cleared his throat. "My name is Jackson. Franklin Jackson. I work for the banking firm of Caudle and Woodson. I have word that you are looking for this Job Toby."

"Yes, I'd like to know where he's at."

"Could we talk in private, sir?"

"Carlos, give me a few minutes with Mr. Jackson."

"Sure."

"Sorry, but this is a very fragile situation," said Jackson. "I received a telegram two days ago from a bank in the New Mexico Territory that money taken in a Kansas robbery had showed up there."

"And?"

"The man who spent this money was Job Toby."

"Where do I fit in?"

"I am getting to that part. Pinkerton wants a fee of fifty percent of the amount recovered from the robbery. Our client and I feel that's too much. The agency will also charge us for numerous expenses."

"Does Pinkerton know this information about the money Toby's spending?"

"No, this is a well-kept secret. We will pay them, of course, for reasonable costs that have been incurred, but not such a high amount."

"Where do I come in?"

"If you could go to New Mexico and recover as much money as you can, we are prepared to pay you twenty-five percent of the recovered amount."

"There are lots of deputy U.S. marshals out there, plus local lawmen, that you could hire to do this job."

"You must realize we don't care about this man being arrested, shot, or whatever. Our intention is to get as much of that money back as possible and before he spends it all."

"What's he doing out there?"

"I understand he's fixing up a building for a saloon and bawdy house."

"What if I fail?"

"Then we can always go back to our first plan and use Pinkerton."

"Simple as all that?"

"Yes. A quarter of a million dollars in cash is a huge sum of money. An unbelievable amount to be stolen. Earl Simpson and his gang may have committed the largest robbery in history, but we want no publication of that amount ever in the press. It would only draw more bees to the honey."

"I understand."

"That is why I came here to find you. People say you're closemouthed and a man who gets things done."

"You know where this Earl Simpson is at now?"

"Staying on a ranch outside Fredericksburg. He's broke. In bad health, they say."

"You don't want him?"

The man shook his head. "He won't admit to anything as long as he's not in court. He has no money to show for it. I understand he crawled on his hands and knees into some fort out there after Toby tortured his men to death and took his money. They must have left him on foot."

"How did you find me?"

"A few twenty-dollar bills with the right serial numbers were cashed close by right here."

Slocum nodded. "That was the money Toby gave Maria here when he left."

"Yes. Then he went to Mexico. From there, we tracked the money to Mesilla and now Silver City, where he must be trying to settle."

"You still never said why you chose me."

"You remember an officer back in the war named Colonel Bryan Gipson?"

"Yes, he was my company commander during part of the war."

"The colonel sits on our board of directors. Your name came up. He speaks very highly of you."

"How did my name come up, if I might ask?"

"Pinkerton filed several reports mentioning your involvement in recovering Mrs. Toby from the Simpson gang. Of course, you weren't aware then about all the money they carried with them."

"No, I wasn't. My man Carlos and I slipped in, got Mrs. Toby out of their camp safely, scattered their horses, and fled. If I'd known they had that kind of money, I'd've woke them up and collected it, too."

"Are you interested in trying to recover the money?"

"If I was sure that she'd be safe here, I'd go see what I could do."

"What do you need?"

"Let me talk to my men here and talk to Mrs. Toby about taking leave. Where can I find you?"

"I'll wait around a few hours, if you don't mind. I think haste in this case is important."

"We had two men come calling on Mrs. Toby about a week ago. She and I were gone at the time. My men said they acted tough. They've not been back, but I can't place who they would be."

"We know Simpson hired a few gunmen, but when he was unable to pay them and the money was obviously gone, they quit him."

"That might have been who it was. They have not been back. Come to the house, I'll introduce you to Mrs. Toby, and I'll start talking to my people."

He took Jackson inside the dwelling and introduced him to Maria and Juliana. Then he went to the barn and talked to Carlos about the boy staying there to look after things while he went to find Toby.

"Won't you need me to go with you?" Carlos asked.

"I need her protected more. I couldn't leave here and not have her guarded by someone I trust."

"I can do that."

"I know that. Thanks, amigo." He clapped the boy on his shoulder—not a boy anymore, he was a real man.

Juliana was not as receptive when he spoke to her in private. Biting her lip to keep things inside, she rambled. "I don't want you to leave me—I need you so much—what will I do?"

"Carlos will be here. He's as good as anyone we could hire. Those young vaqueros would fight a buzz saw for you. They're well armed. You will be safe."

She clung to him. "How soon must you go?"

"Today. He's waiting for my answer and then I'll leave."

Burying her face in his chest, she sobbed. "Why? Why should I lose you?"

He hugged her tight and rocked her on her feet.

"Will you come back?" She raised her wet face to look at him for his answer.

"I'll probably need to ride on."

"Oh, that's what I thought." She sniffed and shook her head in disappointment. "I wish you'd return here."

"I'd like to, but I can't right now."

"God be with you, big man. You know you will always have a place here."

"Thanks, Juliana. It has been lovely being with both of you."

She smiled, then kissed him good-bye.

Half an hour later, his saddle and gear were in Jackson's buggy and they left the 345 in a small fog of dust.

"Here's five hundred dollars for expenses." The man handed him the envelope from inside his coat as he drove. "You need more money, wire me in San Antonio.

"You can catch the westbound stage at Fredericksburg for El Paso and on to Lordsburg. There are two stage lines operating between there and Silver City. May God have pity on your ass."

"Hey, how about my stomach, too?"

"That, too."

They both laughed.

Slocum was aboard the westbound coach that evening as the sunset burned off the last of the day. He had many miles to cover. Somewhere out there was lots of money. One quarter of it was going to be his. That is, if he could even recover part of it.

From El Paso west, it rained on him. Unusual in such a dry land. An unbroken gray overcast covered the great sky, and periodically sheets of rain swept over the coach. Chilly air penetrated the interior, where he huddled under a wool blanket and tried to sleep.

Two salesmen shared the rocking coach and sat opposite him. In Mesilla, a woman joined them for the ride. She looked to be in her thirties. Long black hair—the curled ends on her shoulders looked wet. With a put-out look of exasperation written on her face, she tried to make a nest for herself beside him.

He heard her complaining under her breath, until she ended in a huff on the bench beside him. If she'd been a little more friendly, he would have offered to share the warmth of his blanket with her, but that might have insulted her—so he turned away and tried to sleep. The washboard road made that impossible. When he twisted back, he could see the taffeta material of her long coat was not warding off much cold.

"If you would not be insulted, I'd share my blanket with you," he said as privately as possible.

She looked at him hard, and then at the dark blue blanket. "I accept."

Soon, they were familiarly hip to hip under his cover and he could feel her shivering. He reached over and pulled her against him. For an instant, he thought she might rebel, but she was too cold to resist his warmth. In a short while, their body heat grew and with her relaxing, she fell asleep.

Lucky her. Maybe she was simply exhausted. He felt exhausted himself, only catching winks of sleep in the past three days. The stage crew was busy changing horses at the next station when she awoke.

"Where are we?" she asked sleepily.

"An hour and twenty minutes west of where you got on. A heavy grade getting up here, so this stop was close."

"Oh. I am Bernice Hancock."

"Slocum is my name."

"I'm going to Tucson."

"I'm going to Lordsburg and then Silver City."

"I see."

"You need to use the facilities, you better get off. The driver'll be ready to go shortly."

"You're very kind. I better."

He helped her down, then stood with the mist sweeping his face and stretched his arms over his head. To escape the moisture, he went on the porch. It leaked, but he found a dry spot to stand. Soon she returned, and he helped her back on the stage. After him, the drummers climbed back in. Then the coach leaned as the driver scrambled up the side to take the reins.

With a "heeyah," they were off again. Slocum wondered how Juliana was doing. Under the covers, with his arm around Bernice's shoulder, they went to building the warmth again.

"What kind of work do you do, sir?"

"Punch cows," he said, wondering what else he could say.

"Are you a ranch foreman?"

"Not that high up."

"I find that hard to believe."

"Hard as it is to believe, that's what I do."

"What a waste."

"Cows don't think so."

She laughed, and then elbowed him in the ribs as if to correct him. "Cows don't think."

"How do you know? You ever been a cow?"

"Good heavens, no."

He shrugged. "That's my game and I'm sticking to it."

"What will you do in Silver City?"

Try to regain a man's wealth. "Oh, look around. I hear it's a booming place."

"I imagine it may be. Metals like gold and silver can be profitable. Will you prospect?"

"Is it hard work?"

"I think you are pulling my leg."

"Me?"

She shook her head at him as the coach rocked westward, and a spray of rain came in around the canvas curtains. Cold, stiff, and miserable, he slouched down to try and sleep some more.

24

Toby explained to three Mexicans and two Chinese with wheelbarrows how to load faster and deliver their loads out back to dump in piles. Despite the language barriers, he was making sense with the men. Trash and torn-out debris were piled all over the room's floor waiting for their removal.

His carpenters were making stud walls under Teresa's direction for the cribs in the back. Cleaning this place up was a large enough job. Remodeling was something else. Keeping his construction workforce was hard, too. They preferred to drink rather than work. But they were craftsmen, and he wanted their good work to show in his refurbished building—a saloon and dance hall. Teresa wanted to call it "Whispering Winds."

What man would go to drink at a place with that kind of name, let alone go to find himself some ass there? Teresa was busy hiring some girls. She'd sent letters to El Paso, Fort Worth, Houston, and St. Louis. Everything cost money. He'd let two of his own men go home to see their families in Mexico. She said he should cut them from the payroll. But if he had to flee this town, he'd need all his men again. Apaches were all around Silver City like buzzing rattlers.

Every week, they killed lots of lone prospectors, and even small groups of them.

The army came over, but found no sign of the Apaches. They were like ghosts, but he knew ghosts didn't torture and kill people. This remodeling was like pitching hay without Margie Pitch to spell him. How was she doing without him? She'd spoiled him. Sumbitch. What were those two Chinks over there arguing about now?

Back at the casa, he took a bath to rid himself of all the dust. That damn building was nothing but a sand pile. He was seated in the copper tub of hot water when Teresa brought him a tall glass of whiskey and water. Good stuff.

"You see them damn Chinese arguing about something and then get into a fistfight?" he asked.

"Hmm, you know why?" she replied, standing above him.

He stopped before taking a sip. "No. Why?"

"They all own one fifth of their wife. It was that fella Lu's turn to sleep with her last night, and Ho kept her at his place from the night before instead of letting her go to Lu's."

"They each own one fifth of her?"

"Sure. Chinese brides are expensive to get over here. And only a few come, so they share them."

"Holy shit! I'd never heard of that."

She tousled his hair playfully. "Now you have. The cook says supper will be ready shortly."

"I'll be there."

"Is that lumber you ordered going to be here this week?"

"It better." Stuff he ordered didn't ever come on time. He took a sip of his whiskey. Not bad. He wondered about Juliana—had she ever got to talking? That was all behind him. Being a rancher was a damn sight easier than remodeling a place for a saloon-whorehouse. Besides if the whores were good-looking he might use up all the profits himself. When the whiskey was finished, he climbed out of the tub, sloshed water on the tile floor, and went to drying off.

After supper, he sat on a hammock out back and listened to the crickets. It was near time to go to bed and she was still in there working on those books she kept on their operations. This working all the time wasn't much fun. When they got that damn place going, he was taking off. Do some hunting in the mountains. He'd never shot an elk. They said they were huge deer. Never had any of them in Texas.

"You sleepy?" she asked from the doorway.

"No, but I'm horny as hell."

"Good." She chuckled at him. "You do that in bed, too."

"I'm coming."

Later in the night, he lay on his back in the near darkness and looked at the cloth stretched over the bed to keep the scorpions and vinegaroons on the ceiling from falling on them at night. Was this such a wise idea? Settling in a town?

He could hear her soft breathing beside him. What he needed was some virgin to change his luck. There ought to be some tan-skinned virgin around town that her father would take a hundred bucks for. He'd bought them cheaper than that in Texas.

But money didn't mean anything to these dirty old prospectors. One day they'd be rich, the next morning hung over and broke; then they'd stagger back off and pan out another fortune. That is, if an Apache didn't kill them.

That was why he needed to get his business ready. So they could deposit their money with him.

He rolled over against her small butt and discovered he was still half hard. Better dissolve that. Smiling to himself like a tomcat who'd discovered a willing she-cat, he rolled her over on her back, spread her legs, and climbed aboard. Oh, yeah.

25

With her hand cupped over his ear, Bernice whispered, "Aren't you tired of stage rides? I bet a night in a bed would rest both of us."

Slocum closed his eyes. Her offer sounded heavenly as the stage slowed.

"Are we at the next stop already?" she asked, peeking out from behind the curtain.

"Folks, we're being held up by bandits," the driver announced in a serious-sounding voice.

"Gawdamn!" one of the drummers swore. "They did this two months ago. Same damn spot I bet you as last time."

"Everyone get out here with their hands high," a masked man on horseback announced as he undid the door and flung it back.

The drummers went first and then Bernice. Slocum came last, after sticking his six-gun in the waistband behind his back and under his vest. A west wind slapped him as he saw there was another on horseback holding a rifle on them. The first man climbed off his horse and came over with a gunny-sack in his hand,

"Put all your money, watches, and rings in this sack." He had rolled the sack down to half size, and shook it with his left hand at the first drummer, who was digging in his pockets like a scared man desperate to please the masked one, putting coins and paper money in by the handfuls.

When the horse of the outlaw on foot swung around, shielding them from the one on horseback, Slocum drew his .44, fired, and struck the sack holder in the chest. His knees crumpled and he went down. A rifle bullet smashed into the coach and the holdup man's horse, excited, swung to the left. Slocum put two pieces of hot lead in rapid fire into the second robber's torso. They sounded each time like they'd struck a ripe watermelon. He was pitched off his saddle.

His hands still in the air, the bearded driver said, "I've never seen the likes of that shooting, mister. Jesus, you the law?"

Slocum shook his head and holstered his gun. "You all right, ma'am?"

"Oh, sure," she said. "You do that often?"

"No, ma'am. Folks have better habits than those two have in my part of the country."

She swallowed. "I can see why."

The drummers caught the robbers' horses, and the four of them tied the two bodies over the saddles under the stage driver's supervision. When their horses were hitched to the tailgate, the passengers climbed inside, damp from the drizzle. She held up the blanket for Slocum to join her, and he agreed, grateful for the warmth.

"I'm thinking I'll accept your offer," he said.

"Fine," she said, spreading the blanket over them. "I'm about to lose the ringing in my ears. Your gun is sure loud."

"Sorry, but I couldn't afford to donate my traveling money to those two birds."

"We thank you, too," the red-faced drummer said.

"Wish they had law around here like you, mister. Be a damn sight better place to live."

"It's fine, fellas. You two get the next ones."

They all laughed.

* * *

Lordsburg was a dusty crossroads. Heavy wagons were parked everywhere. Plenty of activity was going on in the saloons. A few gunshots were popped in the air by some drunk. The stage agent sent for the sheriff upon learning about the robbery attempt, then walked over and shook Slocum's hand. "I'm authorized to pay you a two-hundred-dollar reward from the San Antonio-California Stage Line for killing them two. Come over to my office and I'll pay you."

"I'll be right there." Then Slocum spoke to the driver. "Hey, I want my gear taken off, too."

The man was obviously taking Bernice's carpetbag off the tailgate. He nodded, and soon set Slocum's saddle and war bag on the ground.

Shaking Slocum's hand, he gave him an approving look. "You did a helluva job. I hadn't seen it, I'd've never believed it. When that horse swung his butt so he protected all of you from that rifle man, you went to shooting. Man, my heart about quit. Thanks again."

"No problem." Slocum turned to Bernice. "I'm going to check on that reward he spoke about. I'll be right back."

She smiled and dropped her gaze to the boardwalk. "I can wait."

"Good. I won't be long."

"I trust that you won't be."

He winked at her. What a nice distraction. He hurried for the stage office. It would be two hours till sundown. Maybe he'd even get time for a bath and shave.

The next morning, he stood by the open window of their hotel room and listened to the noisy birds outside the window.

"Well, when does your stage leave for Silver City?" she asked, hugging her warm body against his bare back.

"Oh, hours from now."

"Wonderful. Let's climb back in bed."

"And what will you do in Tucson?" he asked, twisting her around in front of him so he could sweep her up in his arms.

"Set up housekeeping for my husband. Entertain his guests and attend any social event that helps his rise in stature in the city's social circle."

"He's a mining engineer, right?"

"Yes. Mostly copper. There are vast deposits of it in Arizona."

He kissed her and she returned his kiss, throwing her arms around his neck. Lovely, lovely lady.

"You and him would not be doing this?" Slocum ventured.

"No. Vance gets his kicks out of young brown-skinned girls. My husband cheats on me on a very regular basis."

"Why don't you leave him?"

"How? I have no money. I'm forty years old. Who wants a used-up divorcée without a dowry? Of course, if he died, I could go see the world on his fortune."

"What if you fell into a large sum of money of your own?"

"Large? What do you mean?"

"As much as, oh—thirty thousand dollars."

"You want my right arm?"

"What if you don't go home, but go with me to Silver City and we can play man and wife for, say, a week?"

"Who are you going to rob?"

"A crook who stole another crook's fortune. I get twenty-five percent of the take."

"How does this work?" Her hand rubbed the upper part of his bare leg.

"That works fine. So I'll make a long story short." He told her about his deal to get the money back, and she laughed. "I'd love to do that."

"What if we don't get the money? There's that chance."

She wrinkled her nose at him and then hugged him hard. "Vance can just wonder what in the hell kept me up here so long."

Mr. and Mrs. "Donald Chester" arrived via the stagecoach the next day in Silver City. They climbed down. He was wearing a new business suit as he showed her to the

President's Hotel, where he rented a suite and ordered up champagne.

The door closed on the bellman, and she rested her butt against the door and giggled. "This will be more fun than anything I've done in years."

"I'd say my sponsor won't mind paying fifty bucks a day for this, if we can get back half of his money."

She whirled around the room like a ballerina. "What do we do next, Donald, dear?"

"Find Job Toby and get close to him."

"How do we do that?"

"First try to find him. I'll go sit in a card game or two tonight and try to find out if he's here and where."

"May I join you?"

"I guess so."

A sly smile crossed her mouth as she wet her lips. "Then take off your silly suit. I want to mess up that fancy bed with you."

"Wonderful. I'd much rather wear you on me than this suit."

She fell on her butt on the bed, laughing so hard she doubled over. Finally recovered, she said, "Vance, my dear husband, you are sure missing a wonderful party."

Things began to unfold by noon the next day when he learned that Mr. and Mrs. Toby were remodeling the old Consuella Store building. Slocum strode down there and found a man who resembled the description of Toby, who he'd never met before, covered in dust and ordering the laborers around.

"Good day, sir," Slocum said.

Toby brushed the flour off his sleeves. "Ain't mucha one here. What can I do for you?"

"I'm new to Silver City. My name is Donald Chester and I was hoping to visit with you about—" He made a swirling sign with his fingers to indicate the project. "About your plans here for this place. Perhaps you and the lady over there could meet me and my wife for supper at the President's Hotel this evening. Say at eight in the private dining room?"

Toby blinked and recovered. "Certainly, Chester. My wife and I will meet you there then."

"Good day, sir."

"Ah, yeah, good day to you, too." He waved good-bye with a salute.

Slocum took his leave of the dust-fogged site, but not before he noticed the two pistoleros armed with rifles in the background. Even in Silver City, Job Toby was taking no chances. Those may have been the same two who tortured the Simpson gang members into revealing where the money was hidden.

Back at the hotel, he told Bernice what he'd done. "If we can make Toby think he's a big man, the pistoleros might not guard him so closely. We need to get an invite inside his residence and then take the money."

She nodded. "Did you meet his so-called wife?"

"No, but I wanted to leave some mystery about this rich man in the white suit who came asking him for information."

"Did he take the bait?"

"He was taken aback some. I was unexpected, and I could see his ego growing. What businessman has ever asked Toby for advice before?"

"I guess none."

Slocum exhaled slowly, then reached out and hugged her around the neck. "We are closer than you would think to collecting our reward."

"Sounds too good to be true."

"We don't have it yet. But once I get inside his house with him, I'll not waste a lot of time. But you need to be careful. Those pistoleros are killers and they won't care if you're a man or a woman, they'd cut your throat."

"I'll be careful."

The supper went well. Mrs. Toby—Teresa—was a straight-backed, thin woman with a swarthy complexion. Slocum guessed her older than Toby, but no doubt she provided most of the brains in his operation. She spoke English with only a slight accent, and her dark eyes missed nothing.

Still, from the look on her face, Slocum could see she was awed by the five-course meal, and Bernice acted perfectly as Slocum's hostess.

"You will have to come to our casa," Teresa said. "I can serve you *cabrito* and border food."

"Oh, my dear," Bernice said. "We'd love that. That would get us in the mood for living here, right, Donald?"

"Oh, yes, my dear."

After supper, he and Toby went out on the veranda and smoked some Cuban cigars.

"You know, Chester, I was raised on a two-bit place down in the hill country," Toby began. "But I've been climbing stairs ever since. Did some ranching, made some money, and I'm going in this business without borrowing one dime."

"That's amazing. A self-made man in these times." Slocum lowered his voice. "Do you trust these banks in town? They look a little shaky to me."

"I don't trust any damn bank. Why, hell." He waved the big cigar in his hand. "They could be robbed any day and your money would vanish."

"Right. Very true. I imagine with all the money you have, you must keep it in a large safe."

"No. I'll show you. No one will ever get my money."

"I didn't bring that much money here, fearing I might be robbed."

"It pays to be careful." Puffed up like a bantam rooster, he drew on the cigar and blew smoke out in the night. "I can lend you some of my men if you ever need a guard."

"Oh, that would be very generous of you. Of course, I would reimburse you for any costs incurred."

"Sure, sure, no problem."

Slocum doubted Toby even understood what he'd said to him. How could he lather him some more? "It was so smart of you to buy that building already built. Did an agent find it?"

"No, I didn't need an agent. I found it all boarded up and

went to find the owner. You know, that's easy. You just go to the courthouse and look it up."

"I can tell you are a real businessman." Slocum shook his head as if amazed. "Went to the courthouse and looked it up. My, my. Well, if I find a deal like that, I'll sure need your help to solve it."

Cigar in his mouth, Toby stood at the rail on the veranda porch under the stars and looked over the lights of Silver City like an emperor of Rome. Somewhere, Slocum had seen a picture of Caesar or one of those Romans doing the same thing—except they'd had an audience down there.

Later, back in their hotel room, Slocum and Bernice did a dance and ordered up a bottle of champagne to celebrate. They had been invited to the Tobys' casa to dine on barbequed young goat the following evening. Toby was doing it up in hill country style. How marvelous, my dear.

They were moving closer to Slocum's goal. Naked in bed, they toasted each other and drank to the better days ahead. They spilled a little on the sheets, but who cared? They climaxed the evening with some slow, grinding sex that wound up in a fury, and then they both fell sound asleep.

The next day, he arranged for a driver and carriage to take them to the Tobys' casa that evening. Bernice went out and had a new dress made for the occasion that cost forty dollars. While they were eating some small crust-less sandwiches that the hotel brought to their room in mid-afternoon, Slocum winked at her.

"From here on, it gets tougher. The bank president is going to be at the bank all night, ready to open the doors if we knock. He will have two shotgun guards as well to back me up. Once that money is in that bank, Toby can beat on the doors all he wants. As far as he's concerned, the money will be gone."

"What if he goes to the sheriff?"

"Then they'll arrest him for the robbery."

"But he has men—"

"That's the tough part. There may be shooting."

"Then I want a gun."

"Bernice, I didn't ask you to help me shoot them."

"I want a gun and ammo."

He folded his arms over his chest. "What can you shoot?"

"A five-shot Lady Smith revolver in .22 caliber."

"I'll go and find you one." Standing up, he made a face at the food left on his plate. "I'd rather have had frijoles."

"Now Donald, dear—" She broke into laughter.

"Last night, that steak smothered in wine sauce at supper was horrible."

Looking haughtily at him, she said, "How will I ever drive the cowboy out of you?"

"I can tell you right now. You won't."

In an hour, he brought back the small five-shot pistol plus ammunition, and she loaded it with dexterity. She was no stranger to the weapon, and he felt satisfied she could handle it.

The time arrived, and they left the hotel to ride in the carriage in the last setting sunlight. The high-stepping horses and the hired driver George, in his black suit, all drew the attention of the gathering mine workers and prospectors getting ready for another evening of hell-raising.

When traffic forced George to draw up, they overheard someone on the boardwalk say, "I'm going to be that gawdamn rich someday."

Bernice winked at Slocum and the coach went on.

The casa was, Slocum found, like a small fort. The carriage swung through the gates and Slocum saw no visible guards. George swung around the circular drive and stopped the horses precisely at the foot of the stairs. Teresa came hurrying out to greet them. Dressed in black, she wore a long skirt, white blouse, and a black vest that hugged her tightly. Someone had piled her hair up with combs. She looked the part. In a stiff-looking new suit, Toby joined them on the porch.

Even at a distance, Slocum could smell the whiskey on

the man's breath. He'd fortified himself for another round of compliments and high praise.

"Come in and have a drink," Toby said, leaving the two women to chatter.

They took the bottle and glasses out in the patio area and sat on benches. The garden had been neglected and not watered enough, but the Chinese lanterns provided illumination and the fire in the pit sent a glow over it all.

"What about some other boomtown?" Toby asked. "You been to any others? I hear there's some that are wide-open and roaring."

"I understood this one had the most outcroppings of gold and silver."

"Yeah, well, I hope it lasts for fifty years. Then I won't give a fuck—I mean I won't care. Sorry for the slip. I've been working them damn workers so long now, I even sound like one."

"You need to take a break. You are absolutely working yourself down."

"Ah, hell, I'm tough. I get it done, I can do what the—what the hell I want and let the money roll in." He downed another glass.

They had supper and the goat was good. Much better than the steak the night before. Toby was getting in his cups. The two men left the women and went back out in the patio garden.

In his hand, Toby had a bottle by the neck and one glass. He was drinking his straight from the neck.

"You—you're a good sumbitch, you know that, Chester? I ain't met many good sumbitches since I got to this place. But you, my amigo, are a good one."

"You were going to show me that safe of yours."

"Yeah. I wouldn't show—just any—body this stuff." He rose and put his hand on Slocum's shoulder for support. "I got more damn money than the mint has. You know that?"

"Oh, I must see that."

"Damn right." Walking unsteadily, he led Slocum to a small toolshed and undid the brass lock. It and the chain fell down. Toby waved aside any concern, and opened the door. Inside the dark room, Toby struck a match to show Slocum the two trunks on the floor.

"Don't tell anyone I've got it, but open that one there."

Slocum raised the lid and under the newly lit match's light, he saw the currency. "Why, you are filthy rich."

"Filthy rich son of a bitch—just like you."

Slocum crowded into him and jerked out the man's .45. "Except for one thing. I'm taking the money to where it belongs. Savvy?"

"What the hell are you, the law?"

"No, my name's really Slocum."

Toby's eyes flew open like he couldn't believe anything. "You—you saved my wife!"

"Now you can get loud and I'll shoot you, or you can behave and live—"

"Toby, what have you done?" Teresa demanded, standing in the doorway of the shed. Then she jerked up taller, and Slocum knew the muzzle of Bernice's .22 had been jabbed into her back.

"No loud noises," Slocum said. "We are going to tie you two up and gag you. The money goes back to the rightful owner. You report it stolen and you will be charged with the robbery. This can be easy or hard. I could cut your throats. Tell me what you want."

"We want to live," Teresa said, looking in disgust at Toby. "You had to show him the money, didn't you?"

"I only wanted—"

"Shut up," she said.

Then, when they were seated on the ground and Bernice was holding them at gunpoint, Slocum went and got George. George readily agreed when Slocum told him there was a hundred dollars for him if he helped Slocum do what he wanted done. They made two trips to move the trunks to the carriage. Going back, Slocum tore down some dusty drapes off a window and used them to bind Toby and Teresa.

The two were tied, gagged, and locked in the shed. Slocum took the keys with him.

George brought the carriage around and they climbed on board. Both Slocum and Bernice held their handguns close at their sides, and they arrived at the bank's side door in ten minutes.

Slocum knocked three times, which was the signal, and the door swung open. Two men armed with shotguns came outside and looked everything over. George and Slocum brought the trunks inside under the supervision of the bank president, and put them on a table in the back office.

"I never seen the likes of this," George said with a grin when Slocum counted him out his hundred.

"Forget you ever saw it."

"I will, sir. I sure will."

Slocum saw Bernice collapsed in a captain's chair and went over to her. "Long time, wasn't it?"

"Scary as hell," she said. "I'm still shaking. Did we get it all?"

"What was left. Crane, the bank president, has sent for help to come in tonight and count it. We get a round figure, then they can make up any difference paid to us later. When the sun comes up, you will be on the Lordsburg stage headed home. They will transfer that money to your Tucson bank. So that they can't rob you getting out of here. Set up your account down there so Vance can't get any of it. You may need a lawyer to do that."

"Why give me half of it?" she asked in a hushed voice.

"I'm not giving you half," he said in a soft voice as he leaned over close to her. "I am giving you all of it."

"But why?"

"I don't need it."

"Yes, you do."

He shook his head and winked at her. "Besides, I have rich friends to care for me."

"I'd rather go off with you than even touch that money."

"Sorry, my lady, that's not an option."

Even if he wanted to take her—and he sure liked her a lot.

26

Two weeks later in Santa Fe, with a wine-soaked Mississippi Crook cigar in his teeth, Slocum stepped out of the cantina onto the dark porch and blew a mouthful of smoke into the night air. The batwing doors creaked behind him, and a voice told him not to turn around.

He didn't.

"You know a man named Franklin Jackson?"

Slocum nodded.

"He's been in town today. Asking lots of questions about where you sleep and your horse."

"And?"

"There is a piebald pacer on the end of the hitch rack belongs to me and he has a fair saddle on him. Give me a bill of sale for your horse and fifty dollars and ride out now. Jackson has men watching the apartment and some more at Frank's Livery."

"Why are you doing all this?" Slocum took the cigar out of his mouth, listening close.

"I need fifty dollars and I like your roan horse."

He threw the cigar away. "I'll make you the bill of sale for the roan and pay you. Why does Franklin Jackson want me?"

"He says you stole lots of money in some deal that was supposed to be all his."

The sumbitch.

Under the stars, Slocum let the pacing horse out going north. The high-stepping black piebald wasn't his choice, but the animal did cover ground. The long wavy mane shook as he chugged northward.

Slocum stopped at the stage station at Emuda, ate some of the fat woman's frijoles and tortillas, grained the horse while he feasted, and left in thirty minutes. The sun was trying to come up as he wound his way up the canyon of the Rio Grande Gorge.

So the whole plan to get the money back was to have been a double cross by Jackson. Slocum had fooled Jackson by putting the money in the bank—no way for Jackson to get his hands on it. Now that he knew the man's intentions, Slocum figured that Jackson had expected him to deliver it to him—then he could have shot Slocum and ridden on. In any case, the money was now out of Jackson's reach. Bernice had it in her account and Jackson had no idea who she was. He was sure wrong if he thought he'd get it from Slocum.

How many men would he send after Slocum? Some watching his newfound lover's apartment, others the stables. Two at each place plus Jackson made a total of five. He could lose them in the mountains ahead, even ambush them, but better yet, he'd like to find out Jackson's real plans for the reward.

There were some Jacarillo Apaches he knew lived somewhere north in the big timber. They'd be hard to find this time of year, but he might be able to. Captain Cooke's band.

If he located them, he might hide out all summer with them up there until Jackson ran out of money and went home.

He set the pacer back in gear, and ate up some more of northern New Mexico's wagon road to Colorado. The fast-stepping horse had enough endurance to cover lots of country. Why the man on the saloon porch wanted to trade him for the roan was beyond Slocum. What did he say? He needed the fifty dollars?

That evening, Slocum stopped off at a small trading post where several freighters were parked, bought a two-dollar wool blanket to sleep under, a used Spencer .50 caliber, and 250 rounds of ammo plus ten tubes. The repeater had been well cleaned, oiled, and was in good condition, worth the twelve bucks he paid for it. The man's wife fed him elk stew and corn bread for a quarter, and her bitter coffee beat no coffee at all.

"You know Captain Cooke?" he asked the trader, who came by and sat down on the bench with him.

"Everyone knows him."

"But do you know where I can find him?"

"I can't tell you where he is, but I have a man will tell him you want to talk to him, huh?"

Slocum blew on another steaming coffee the man's wife had just brought. "Tell him Slocum wants to palaver."

"Slocum? I got it. Stick around. He wants to talk, he'll send you word."

Slocum gave the horse a nose bag with corn in it, and hobbled him on the hillside above the store building where the grass grew between the large stumps. This country was covered in mature pine timber; many trees were five and six feet across. A paradise, the Apaches called it. The marshy meadows provided grass and water for their horses. And lots of huge elk summered above the timberlines. Deer in the woods and bear, too—although the Apache were superstitious about the bear. They believed the bear could read people's minds.

"Don't say nothing about him. He will know what you say and meet you on the trail and eat you," High Bird had told him. The Apaches didn't eat the cutthroat trout, either which left the fishing for the hungry white man.

Slocum kicked the sticks and trash out for a place to lie down. And with his .44 beside his head, he put his head down, all wrapped in the blanket, and went to sleep. He was never sure when she arrived or found him.

"That gawdamn blanket is big enough for two," she said, loud enough they could have heard her in Colorado. On her knees, she was grunting, using both hands to unroll him.

"That you, Minnie?" he asked, trying to wake up. It must be in the middle of the night. "Take it easy, we can share this blanket."

He sat up and combed his hair back with his fingers. "How did you know I was here?"

"Apaches know everything about this land. Who comes. Who goes. Everything."

"That's good to know."

She spread the blanket out once he got off it. Then she folded it in two and laid it out. "Now you get on it."

He lay on the open half on his side. She kneeled down and lay on her side with her back to him. Then she whipped the blanket over them and nested her butt in his belly.

In a minute, she was shedding her many-pleated skirt, wiggled out of it and tossed it out from under the covers. He heard the conchos sewed on it ring when it hit the ground. She put her butt back against him. He threw his arm and hand over the top of her to cup the small sag in her belly. In response, she squirmed some. Then he reached under her blouse and played with her firm breasts, making the nipples point like round pepples.

"We're not going to get any sleep that way." She rolled over on her back.

"Why do you think that?"

She giggled. All Indian women giggled when they got caught, or were amused, or even when they were embarrassed.

He climbed over to get between her legs. "This why you came here?"

"I didn't want to miss nothing." She pulled him down to kiss her. When he finally broke off, he raised up to look down at her. She sighed. "That is why I came. Indians don't kiss their women."

He reached under and inserted his growing erection in her. "I've got all kinds of kisses."

She clutched his forearms and raised her butt to let him go deeper. Hell, who wanted to sleep anyhow?

At dawn, she was busy cooking on a small fire. Small strings of elk meat he figured she'd either brought, or gone and gotten from the store on his new account. Charged on his account because she didn't have one. Oh, well. He raised up and sat cross-legged. He had a camp girl as long as he wanted Minnie.

He caught some trout in the sparkling stream beyond the store with some worms he drove out of the ground by pounding on some stakes. Catgut line on a willow pole, steel hook with plump red worm on it, drifting into a brush pile that diverted the rushing stream—and bam! Two sixteen-inchers in less than ten minutes. Life was hard up in this high country. Hard to leave.

She picked the way riding a three-dollar pony he bought for her from another Apache. They wandered through the meadow valleys, saw several big elk, and even a grizzly. The silver-tip went on west, loping off though the willows, and Slocum didn't miss him. Grizzlies could be terrors.

He shot a small doe, so they didn't waste too much meat, plus she was fat and tender. Must have lost her fawn earlier and that put the meat on her. Then, one day when they were camped on Turnip Creek, he saw a half dozen armed raiders coming off the mountain. They had on unblocked stovepipe hats, and some wore red bandannas. Blousy white cotton Mexican pullover shirts and breechclothts.

Under his derby hat, Captain Cooke rode up and grinned big. *"Yut-ta-hey sa-comie."*

"Yut-ta-hey yourself. How have you been been?"

"Fine." Cooke beat on his chest with his fists. "And you?"

"Good enough."

"Who is this man follows you?" Cooke gave a head toss to the southeast.

"He wants my money."

"You got lots of money?" Cooke grinned big.

"No, but he thinks so."

"What will he do when he finds you?"

"Oh, kill me probably."

"Not on Jacarillo Apache land. We like our friends, don't we, Minnie?"

She looked up from cooking and nodded with a big smile.

"I say we surround his camp tonight and wake him up. Then we take his horses and send him home."

"Can I talk to him when you catch him?" Slocum asked.

"Sure."

"Good. When do we go after him?"

"In a little while after sun dies."

He'd have his day or night with Jackson after all. They must have gotten closer than he'd even imagined. Nice to have influential friends in high places.

So they set out under the stars, Cooke in the lead. Slocum rode in the middle because white eyes did not see as good as Indians at night.

"Where did you get that black and white horse?" Cooke asked over his shoulder.

"Santa Fe. A man needed fifty dollars."

"You buy him for that?"

"I threw in a good roan horse."

Cooke laughed.

Past midnight, they dismounted a ways away and crept up on the campfire's glow. Cooke pointed out each snoring man, and soon one of his men stood poised over each of them. Then he kicked a man in a bedroll, and he woke up with a start. Cooke's big knife was against his jugular vein in a flash.

"Why are you on Apache lands?"

"I'm looking for an outlaw. I-I have—want no trouble with your people."

"Is this the man?"

Jackson swallowed hard and his eyes bugged out in the firelight's soft orange glow. "That you, Slocum?"

"Been waiting for you, Jackson. Guess you brought my expense check?"

"You bastard!"

"Here, here, these Indians don't cuss. You got me to go get the money for you, and then you were going to keep it all, right?"

"Not exactly."

"I put the money in your firm's name, didn't I?"

"Why, I don't know. You dumb bastard. We both could have been rich."

"I could have been pushing up daisies, too, and you'd've kept it all."

"No, get it back and make a fair split with me."

"I gave my share to a good cause. I ain't getting it back. I didn't want it. I figured the man who lost it got about half of his money back, which beat your system."

"All right, what are you going to do with us?"

"They wanted to hang your hair in their lodges. I said no. Take off your boots, socks, and pants. We're taking all you have on you and you can walk back to Santa Fe bare-assed and barefooted."

"You ain't leaving us even one gun?"

"Nope. But you'll be damn tough by the time you get back to civilization."

"I'll find you, Slocum. Gawdamn you, I'll find you."

Slocum moved in with a stiff uppercut to the jaw and knocked him down on his ass. "Don't forget, next time I'll gun your sorry ass down if you come after me. There won't be no talking, nothing, but the last thing you'll hear is the blast of my Colt."

Slocum walked to where the Apache bucks were shaking the money out of boots and pants. He squatted down and picked up a handful of folding money. Fives, tens, and twenties. "These are for Minnie. Captain Cooke, the rest is yours."

"You're sure spoiling her," Cooke said.

Slocum laughed, going for his horse. "She needs a lot of spoiling."

In the fall, Slocum was riding back through the Texas hill country. He'd been by to see Juliana, but Maria said she was in San Antonio getting a wedding dress fitted for that upcoming event.

"What should I tell her?" Maria asked, wringing her hands.

"Nothing. If she's found a good man, she doesn't need to know I was even by here."

"Oh, he's a good hombre. He has two small boys. And has a ranch on the San Saba, but he is moving over here."

Slocum smiled at her. "God bless them."

It was one of those sunny warm days, and at midmorning he was riding on into Decore. Then he recalled how Margie Pitch had said she went home to lunch early for a couple of hours most every day. That was how he'd trapped old Kelso. Slocum went off up the creek road and came in through the willows. Hitched his dun horse in the thicket and headed for the back door.

She came out the back door and threw a bucket of scraps out to the chickens, who flocked from all over and squawked, charging in for their share. When she looked up, she blinked.

"Slocum?"

He took off his hat and wiped his sweaty forehead on his sleeve. "I've been called worse."

A smile of disbelief swept her face. "I sure never figured you'd ever come back by. Let alone to see me."

"See how wrong you can be?" He climbed the steps and took her chin in his hand. Then he kissed her.

She hugged his waist and dragged him inside the kitchen. "Now tell me you have to run."

He put his hat on the ladder-back chair post. "Why, I've got all day."

She chuckled and hooked her arm in his to lead him off. "So have I. Let's start upstairs."

"I couldn't have said it any better myself."

Later, she showed him the newspaper articles about how Job Toby had been killed in a mine cave-in near Silver City, and another about how Earl Simpson had taken his own life after having another stroke.

At mid-afternoon, he headed his dun horse for San Antonio. There would be some brown-skinned girls dancing and singing in those Alamo sidewalk cantinas. He loved them all.

Watch for

SLOCUM AND THE GIFT HORSE

374th novel in the exciting SLOCUM series
from Jove

Coming in April!

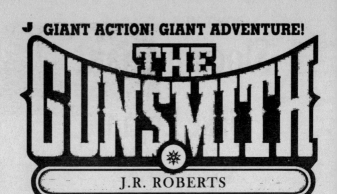

GIANT ACTION! GIANT ADVENTURE!

THE GUNSMITH

J.R. ROBERTS

Little Sureshot And
The Wild West Show
(Gunsmith Giant #9)

Dead Weight
(Gunsmith Giant #10)

Red Mountain
(Gunsmith Giant #11)

The Knights of Misery
(Gunsmith Giant #12)

The Marshal from Paris
(Gunsmith Giant #13)

Lincoln's Revenge
(Gunsmith Giant #14)

penguin.com/actionwesterns